TRAPPED IN A WORLD OF TOTAL TECHNOLOGY

Ted Kennedy is caught in a world where mining the moons of Jupiter is routine, but looking carefully at man's motivations is frowned upon when—infrequently—it's attempted.

Ted is brought face-to-face with impending genocide—and must decide whether or not to attempt to undermine the plan, making himself a fugitive in a hostile world!

"AN EXCELLENT YARN ON ALL COUNTS, AND THE PICTURE OF NEW YORK'S TWENTY-FIRST CENTURY EQUIVALENT OF MADISON AVENUE IS SOLID—BETTER THAN THE POHL-KORNBLUTH SPACE MERCHANTS, IN FACT."

P. Schuyler Miller,
Astonishing Science Fiction

INVADERS FROM EARTH

ROBERT SILVERBERG

AN AVON BOOK

AVON BOOKS
A division of
The Hearst Corporation
959 Eighth Avenue
New York, New York 10019

First Avon Printing, July, 1968

Cover illustration by Don Crowley

Printed in the U.S.A.

For Boggs and Grennell—
The Deans of Science Fiction

1

TED KENNEDY had a premonition the night before. It came, as so many premonitions do, in the form of a dream. Guns blazed, innocent people died, fire spread over the land. Looming thermonuclear mushrooms hung in the skies. He stirred fitfully, sighed, nearly awoke, and sank back into sleep. But when morning came he felt pale and weary; he ended the insistent buzz of the alarm with an impatient wrist-snap and dangled his legs over the edge of the bed, rubbing his eyes. The sound of splashing water told him that his wife was already awake and in the shower.

He had never awakened easily. Still groggy, he shambled across the bedroom to the cedar chest, groped for his robe, and headed for the kitchen. He punched buttons on the autocook, setting up breakfast. One of these mornings, he thought wryly, he'd be so sleepy he'd order steak sandwiches on toast instead of the usual bacon.

Marge was out of the shower and drying herself with all her awesome early-morning vigor when he returned to the bedroom to dress.

"Breakfast up?" she asked.

Kennedy nodded and fumbled in the closet for his best suit, the dark green one with red lace trim. He would need to look good today; whatever the conference on Floor Nine was, it was bound to be important, and it wasn't every day a third-level public relations man got summoned to Floor Nine.

"You must have had a bad dream last night," Marge said suddenly. "I can tell. You're still brooding over it."

7

"I know. Did I wake you up?"

She smiled, the bright sudden smile that so astonished him at 5 A.M. They had always been different that way— he the late riser who was still fresh long past midnight; she buoyant and lively from the earliest morning hours till the middle of the evening. "You didn't wake me up, no. But I can see the dream's still with you. Tell me about it—and hurry up. You don't want to miss the car pool."

"I dreamed we were at war," he said.

"War? With whom?"

He hesitated. "I don't know. I mean, I don't remember any of the motivation. But it was a terrible war . . . and I have the nagging feeling *we* started it."

"How could there possibly be a war? Everyone's at peace, darling! It's been that way for years. There aren't going to be any more wars on Earth, Ted."

"Maybe not on Earth," he said darkly.

He tried to laugh it off, and by the time he had finished breakfast some of the irrational fear-tide had begun to re-cede. They ate quietly. Kennedy was never much of a breakfast-table conversationalist. It was nearly 6 A.M. by the time they finished and Marge had dumped the dishes into the washer; the sun was rising now over the low Con-necticut hills. He finished dressing, tugging at his collar to keep his braided throat-cord from throttling him, and gave his epaulets a light dusting of powdered gold. Marge re-mained in her gown; she worked at home, designing house furnishings and draperies.

At 6:18 sharp he was on the porch of his home, and at 6:20 the shiny yellow '44 Chevrolet-Cadillac drew up outside, Alf Haugen at the wheel. Haugen, a stocky, meaty-faced man with bright sharp eyes, worked at the desk behind Kennedy's in the Steward and Dinoli office, and this was his week to drive the car-pool auto. Of the six of them, Haugen had by far the best car, and he enjoyed flaunting it.

Kennedy half-trotted down the walk to Haugen's car. He glanced back and waved at Marge, noting with some an-noyance that she had gone out on the porch wearing only her filmy morning gown. Some of the men in the car were bachelors, and, unlike Haugen, Kennedy didn't believe in flaunting his treasures openly. Marge was a handsome woman, but he felt no urge to demonstrate that fact to

8

Lloyd Presslie or Dave Spalding, or to any of them for that matter.

He slid into the back of the car; Presslie and Mike Cameron moved over to make room for him. Haugen nudged the start-button, the turboelectrics thrummed, and the car headed smoothly off toward the city.

Apparently, Spalding had been in the middle of some joke when they stopped to pick up Kennedy. Now he reached the punch-line and the five of them, everyone in the car but Kennedy, laughed.

Kennedy disliked Spalding. The slim young fourth-level man lived in the apartment development three miles further along the road; he was unmarried, deeply intense about most subjects, and almost never let anyone know what he might actually be thinking. It was not a trait that endeared him to people, which was probably why he was still only a fourth-level man after three years at Steward and Dinoli. It was no secret that old Dinoli preferred outgoing types, married, in his higher levels.

"Any of you know anything about the big deal brewing today?" Mike Cameron asked suddenly.

Kennedy jerked his head to the left. "What big deal? Did you get invited to Floor Nine, too?"

Cameron nodded. "We all were. Even Spalding. I guess Dinoli sent that memo to the whole third and fourth level yesterday afternoon. Something big's brewing, mark my words, friends!"

"Maybe the agency's dissolving," Lloyd Presslie suggested sourly. "Or maybe Dinoli hired a bunch of top-level men away from Crawford and Burstein and we're all being bounced down three notches."

Haugen shook his head. "It's some big new account the old man landed. I heard Lucille talking about it near closing time. Whenever you're in doubt, ask Dinoli's secretary." He laughed coarsely. "And if she's reluctant to spout, pinch her a little."

The car swung into the main artery of the Thruway. Kennedy peered pensively out the window at the towns flashing by, a hundred feet below the gleaming white ribbon of the main road. He said little. The thunderburst of H-bombs echoed in his ears, souvenir of the past night's dreaming, and in any event he still felt drugged by sleep.

Some big new account. Well, even so, that shouldn't

9

affect him. He had started handling public relations for Federated Bauxite Mines only last week—a long-range project whose ultimate aim was to convince the people of a large Nebraska district that their economy wouldn't be upset and their water supply polluted by the local aluminum-seekers who had newly invaded their district. He had just scarcely begun preliminary research; they wouldn't yank him off the account so soon.

Or would they?

There was no predicting what Dinoli might do. Public relations was a tricky, fast-moving field, and its province of operations was expanding all the time.

Kennedy felt strangely tense, and for once the smooth purr of the throbbing generators beneath him failed to ease his nerves.

It was 6:52 A.M. when Haugen's car rolled off the Thruway and rode down the long slanting ramp that led into upper Manhattan. At 6:54 the car had reached the corner of 123rd and Lenox, in the heart of the business district. The gleaming white tower that housed Steward and Dinoli was before them. They left the car, Haugen turning it over to attendants who would park it on the second floor of the building.

At 6:57 they were in the elevator; by 6:59, they had reached the front door of Steward and Dinoli, and precisely at 7 A.M. Kennedy and his five car-pool companions were at their desks.

Kennedy's working day lasted from 7:00 to 2:30. This year, by city ordinance, public relations and advertising men worked early shift; come January 1, 2045, they would move up an hour to the 8 A.M. group. Only a stagger-system such as this prevented frightful congestion in the enormous city. To have every worker in the city report to his office and leave at the same hour was unthinkable.

Kennedy's desk was neatly arranged, as he had left it yesterday afternoon. The memo from Mr. Dinoli lay pigeon-holed in the catchall to his right; he unspindled it and read through it again.

> *Floor Nine*
> *2:12* P.M.

Dear Theodore:
Would you be good enough to come downstairs to

my office tomorrow morning, at 9 o'clock or there-
abouts? A matter of some urgency is on the docket,
and I think you're one of the men who can help.

Thanks—and best to your wife. We ought to get
together more often socially.
LD:lk

Lou

Kennedy smiled and dropped the note into his ready
file. He was hardly fooled by the cheery tone or by the
affable "Lou"; Dinoli amused himself by keeping up a
first-name relationship with the second- and third-level
men, but Kennedy knew he had as much chance of ever
seeing the agency head socially as he did of becoming a
star center-fielder for a big-league baseball team. There
was a certain gulf, and that gulf was *never* bridged.

The casual "or thereabouts" in the note was to be ignored, Kennedy knew: he arrived at Floor Nine at 9 A.M.
sharp, or else he bounced back to fifth-level in a hurry.
You learned punctuality around Dinoli.

The morning passed slowly; Kennedy was expecting a
telestat report on the situation in Nebraska from one of
the agency's field operatives, but this wasn't due to arrive
until one. To kill time, he doodled up a few possible opening gambits for the campaign there, centering them
around a standard point of reference: What's Good For
Big Corporations (in this case, Federated Bauxite) Is Very
Good For You.

His mind wasn't fully on his work, though. By 8:15 he
realized he wasn't going to get anything done on the current project until he'd had that meeting with Dinoli, and
he shut up his folders and filed them away. There was no
sense working on a project with his mind clogged by anxi-
ety. Public relations was a difficult job and Kennedy took
it seriously, as he took most other things.

At five to nine he shoved back his rollchair, locked his
desk, and crossed the floor to Alf Haugen's desk. Haugen
had already shut up shop; there was a look of keen ex-
pectancy on his heavy-jowled face.

"Going down to see Dinoli?" Haugen asked casually.

Kennedy nodded. "It's pushing 9 A.M. The old man
wouldn't want us to be late."

Together they walked down the brightly lit office, past

11

the empty desks of Cameron and Presslie, who apparently had already gone downstairs. They emerged in the less attractive outer office where the fourth-level men worked, and there Spalding joined them.

"I guess I'm the only one on my level going," he whispered confidentially. "None of the others are budging from their desks, and it's two minutes to nine."

They crossed the hall to the elevator bank and snared a downgoing car. Kennedy saw that the four private offices in which the agency's second-level men worked were dim and unlit; that probably meant they had spent the entire morning with Dinoli.

Steward and Dinoli occupied four floors of the building. Dinoli's office (Steward had long since been eased out of control, and indeed out of any connection whatsoever with the firm) was at the bottom of the heap, taking up all of Floor Nine. Floor Ten was the agency's library and storage vault; Kennedy worked on Eleven, and the fifth-, sixth-, and seventh-level underlings labored in the crowded little cubicles on Floor Twelve.

The elevator opened into a luxurious oak-paneled foyer on Floor Nine. A smiling secretary, one of Dinoli's flock of bosomy young females, met them there. "You have an appointment with the chief," she said, not asking but telling. "Won't you come this way?"

She led them, Kennedy first, followed by Haugen and Spalding, through the vast salon which served Dinoli by way of a vestibule and waiting room, then into the narrower corridor where tiny television cameras studied them as they approached. Kennedy heard relays click shut as he went past; the spy-system had passed on him, it seemed.

Dinoli's office door was a thick plank of rich-grained oak, in which a tiny gold plaque reading *L. D. Dinoli* was deeply inset. The door swung open as they drew near.

The vista thus revealed had always seemed breathtaking to Kennedy. Dinoli's private office was a room five times as long as it was broad, which seemed to swing away into the reaches of infinity. A giant picture window, always immaculate, gave access to a panoramic view of Manhattan's bustling streets.

Dinoli himself sat at the head of a long, burnished table. He was a small, piercing-eyed man of sixty-six, his face lean and fleshless and surmounted by a massive hook of a nose. Wrinkles spread almost concentrically from that mighty nose, like elevation-lines on a geological contour map. Dinoli radiated energy.

"Ah, gentlemen. Won't you come in and be seated." Again, statements, not questions. His voice was a deep black-sounding one, half croak and half boom.

Immediately at Dinoli's right and left hands sat the agency's four second-level men. Dinoli, of course, occupied the lofty eminence of the first level alone. After the second-level boys came those of the third: Presslie, Cameron, and four others. Kennedy took a seat near Cameron, and Haugen slipped in across the table facing him. Spalding sat to Kennedy's right. He was the only jarring figure in the otherwise neat pyramid, which began with Dinoli, sloped to the four second-level men, and was based on the eight third-level executives.

"We're all here, then," Dinoli said calmly. The clock over his head, just above the upper rim of the picture window, read 9:00:00. It was the only clock Kennedy had ever seen that gave the time in seconds elapsed, as well as minutes and hours. "Gentlemen, I'd like you to meet our new clients, if you will." His clawlike forefinger nudged a button on the elaborate control panel near his hand.

A rear door opened. Three elegant men in crisp green full-dress executive uniforms entered, stiffly erect, conscious of their rank and bearing. They were cold-eyed, hard-looking men. Poised, mildly contemptuous of their hosts, they stood by the door.

"Our newest clients," Dinoli announced. "These gentlemen are from the Extraterrestrial Development and Exploration Corporation, Ganymede Division."

Despite himself, Kennedy shuddered faintly. The image of crashing cities flickered once again before his eyes, and he wondered if perhaps his premonition had held some truth.

13

2

DINOLI LOOKED marvelously proud of himself. His beady eyes darted here and there through the room, fixing on each man at least once, as he prepared to deliver himself of the details of his latest coup.

Kennedy had to feel a sharp twinge of admiration for the savage old battler. Dinoli had clawed himself to first rank in public relations by sheer vigorous exertion, coupled with some judicious backstabbing; to be affiliated at all with him, whether on third-level or sixth, was a measure of distinction in the field.

"Executive Second-Level Hubbel of Public Liaison. Executive Second-Level Partridge of Public Liaison. Executive Second-Level Brewster of the Corporation's Space Expeditionary Command." Dinoli indicated each of the men with a quick birdlike hand gesture.

Kennedy studied them. Hubbel and Partridge were obviously desk men, fiftyish, well built and on the stout side, both of them deeply, and probably artificially, tanned. They looked formidably competent.

Brewster was a different item, though. Short and compact, he was a dark-faced little man who stood ramrod straight, hard, cold eyes peering at the group out of a lean, angular face. He looked tough, and the heavy tan on his cheeks was convincing.

Of course! Kennedy thought, with a sudden shock of wonder. *The space explorer!*

"As members of my staff," Dinoli said, "you all know well that anything you may be told in the confines of this room is absolutely confidential. I trust that's understood, gentlemen. Otherwise get out."

Thirteen heads went up-down affirmatively.

14

"Good. May I say by way of preface that this is perhaps the biggest and most important job Steward and Dinoli has ever handled—perhaps the biggest S and D will *ever* handle. Every PR firm in the nation was canvassed for this job before we landed the contract. I needn't add that successful handling of this new account will result in substantial upward alterations in the individual status increments of those men working on it."

Dinoli paused a long moment. The old man was a master of the dramatic approach. He said at length, "To fill you in on the background, first: Executive Brewster has recently returned from a space journey sponsored by his Corporation. The Major was connected with the Mars expedition, of course, and with the less successful Venus mission that preceded it—and I might add that his heroism was a major factor in minimizing losses on the unfortunate Venus encounter. Executive Brewster's third and most recent Corporation-sponsored mission was to Ganymede—which is, of course, the largest of the moons of our great planetary neighbor Jupiter."

Kennedy wrinkled his brows in surprise; Dinoli seemed to catch the expression, and shot a terrifying glance at him. The old man said smoothly, "The existence of this third interplanetary mission is still secret. The poor publicity aroused by the Venus mission was a factor influencing the Corporation to suppress information to the Ganymede trip until its successful conclusion."

Dinoli made an almost imperceptible gesture and a motion-picture screen unreeled itself in the back of the great room. "Executive Brewster has brought us a film of his activities on Ganymede. I'd like all of us to see this film before we go any further in this meeting."

Two of Dinoli's young undersecretaries appeared, pushing a sliding table on which was mounted a movie projector. One girl deftly set up the projector while another pressed the control that would opaque the picture window. The room grew dim; Dinoli signaled and the remaining lights were extinguished. Kennedy turned in his seat to see the screen.

The projector hummed.

A PRODUCTION OF THE EXTRATERRES-

said the opening title, against a pulsing background of red, white, and blue. Credit-lines followed. And then, quite suddenly, Kennedy found himself staring at an alien landscape, oddly quiet, oddly disturbing.

Bleak whiteness confronted him: the whiteness of an almost endless snowfield, beneath a pale blue sky. Jagged mountain ranges, rock-bare and snow-topped, loomed in the distance. Clouds of gray-green gas swirled past the eye of the camera.

"This is the surface of Ganymede," came the attractively resonant voice of Brewster. "As you can see, frozen ammoniamethane snow covers the ground in most areas. Ganymede, of course, is virtually planetary in size—its diameter is thirty-two hundred miles, which is slightly more than that of Mercury. We found the gravitation to be fairly close to that of Earth, incidentally. Ganymede's a heavy-core planet, probably torn out of Jupiter's heart at the time the system was formed."

As he spoke, the camera's eye moved on, and Kennedy's with it: on to examine the fine striations in an outcropping of rock, on to peer down at a tiny, determined lichen clinging to the side of an upthrust tongue of basalt.

Suddenly the camera whirled dizzyingly upward for a look at the sky. Kennedy was jolted. Jupiter filled a vast segment of the sky, a great heavy ball hanging like a brooding giant just above.

"Ganymede was about six hundred and fifty thousand miles distant from Jupiter at the time of this film's making," Brewster said dryly. "At this distance Jupiter takes up quite a chunk of the heavens."

Kennedy stared uneasily at the monstrous cloud-wrapped planet, whose velvety pearl-gray surface gave hint of unimaginable turbulence deep beneath the outer band of atmosphere. To his relief, the camera finally left the huge world and returned to the Ganymedean landscape.

For perhaps five minutes more the film drifted on over the lonely, bleak land. Then eight spacesuit-clad figures appeared, faces nearly hidden behind their breathing masks, bodies shrouded by the metal-impregnated suits.

"The members of the expedition," Brewster commented.

The camera panned to a spaceship, standing slim and tall on a bare patch of rock. The ship bore dark green numerals painted on its shining silver flank.

"The expeditionary ship," Brewster said.

After a survey of the outer skin of the ship from various angles, and a few more glimpses of the spacesuit-clad crewmen, the camera shifted to pick up a strangely cold-looking pool of greasy liquid.

"One of the occasional Ganymedean paraffin lakes," said Brewster.

The camera skirted the pool's edge, doubled back through a snowfield, and centered suddenly on four weird figures—four creatures vaguely man-shaped, their faces noseless, their eyes hooded by folds of flesh. They were pale white in color, hairless, virtually naked except for some sort of woven cloth girdle round their middles. They were staring sadly at the camera, faces devoid of any understandable expressions.

"These are the natives of Ganymede," Brewster remarked blandly.

Brewster had certainly underplayed it. It took three or four seconds for the effect of his quiet words to make itself known, and then Kennedy felt as if he'd been bashed in the stomach by a battering ram. He had been watching the film intently enough, but superficially—observing it in a detached manner, since the mere sight of alien landscapes was not enough to involve him deeply. But now, suddenly, to have alien life sprung on him. . . .

The Venus expedition had been a dismal failure, mechanical difficulties making it nearly impossible for the explorers to cope with the formaldehyde soup that was Venus' atmosphere. But in their short stay they had definitely verified the fact that there was no animal life on the second planet.

Mars, too, had proved barren, despite the hopes of many. A few lichens, a few podded weeds that survived in the near vacuum, but nothing else. Humanity, and Ted Kennedy, had begun to decide that man was alone in the Solar System, and possibly in the universe.

And now, suddenly—

"The Ganymedeans are a primitive people living in sprawling villages of a few thousand inhabitants each," Brewster said, in a standard travelogue manner. "They seem to cover the entire land mass of Ganymede, which is distributed over three continents. We estimated their numbers at about twenty-five million."

Moistening his lips, Kennedy stared at the four alien beings against the alien backdrop of methane snow. He still had no idea what possible tie-in Dinoli had with all this, but he was waiting.

"During our stay," Brewster went on, "we learned the rudiments of their language. It's a fairly simple agglutinating tongue, and our linguists are at work on it now. We discovered that the Ganymedeans have a working clan system, with sharp tribal rivalries, and also that they show neither any particular fear or any liking for us. The expeditionary geologist's report shows that Ganymede is exceptionally rich in radioactive minerals. Thank you."

The film came abruptly to its end with the last word of Brewster's sentence. The light went on, dazzling Kennedy's eyes; the secretaries appeared from somewhere, deopaqued the big window, and wheeled the projector out. The screen vanished into its recess in the ceiling.

In less than a minute the room was as it had been before. But none of its occupants were quite the same.

Dinoli leaned forward, his eyes glittering brightly. "I think you begin to see the magnitude of what's unfolding before us, men."

Kennedy squirmed uneasily in his contour chair. He saw some of the implications—particularly in that punchline Brewster had tacked on to his little travelogue. *The expeditionary geologist's report shows that Ganymede is exceptionally rich in radioactive minerals.*

The way he had said it as a *non sequitur* made the fact seem almost irrelevant. Kennedy had a good ear for seeming irrelevancies; ultimately, they often turned out to be of critical importance in the case.

Dinoli glanced at the taller and fatter of the two liaison men and said, "Now, Executive Hubbel, will you fill my men in on some of the implications to be drawn from this situation on Ganymede?"

Hubbel coughed ostentatiously. "You've seen the existence of alien life on this planet-sized moon. You've seen also that Ganymede holds exceptional mineral wealth, which our Corporation proposes to mine in the name of the public good by virtue of our U.N. charter agreement.

18

We've gone to considerable expense developing and outfitting ships to explore space, and naturally we're counting on recouping our expenditures on Ganymede. Partridge?"

The other blinked like a sleepy cougar and said smoothly, "We feel there may be certain difficulties in obtaining mining rights from the Ganymedeans."

Suddenly Kennedy began to understand. He felt a muscle in his right calf start to quiver.

Dinoli grinned triumphantly. "Here's where *we* come in, boys. There might be conflict—conflict with the obstinate Ganymedeans. Some people might call that a war of aggression. Actually, of course, it's sheer *necessity*. We need what Ganymede has; the Corporation has sunk billions into opening up space for humanity. You understand this. You're all clever men. That's why you work here instead of for a second-rate outfit."

Partridge said, "Naturally, the people might not sympathize with our plea of necessity. They might think we were imperialistic."

"This impression would of course have to be counteracted by careful public relations management," Hubbel said thoughtfully, putting a cap on the whole thing.

"And we've been chosen to handle it," finished Dinoli.

That was it. That was all there was to it.

Kennedy kept his face blank of emotional reaction. The "agency mask," Marge called it privately. What Marge didn't know was that frequently the agency mask hid an equal blankness of inner feeling. Kennedy suspended judgment, waiting to hear more.

"We plan an intensive world-wide blanketing," Dinoli said. "These gentlemen will be working closely with us at all times. Specific target dates have already been set up. There's a date on which first knowledge of the existence of life on Ganymede will be given to the public—almost immediately, I can tell you—and there's a terminal date on which the occupation force will have to be put down to assist the Corporation. Between those dates, it'll be our responsibility to handle the campaign."

Dinoli leaned back, grinning expansively. "Our constitution provides that no more than four men may be second-level at any one time in our organization. However, we're a flexible group. For the duration of this campaign, those of you who are third-level will draw second-level salaries,

19

without formal advancement in rank. You second-level boys will get salary boosts as well. As for you, Dave Spalding—you'll draw third-level pay, while officially remaining a fourth-level man. Whether these boosts become permanent or not depends largely on the success of the campaign." The old man's eyes traveled down the rows. "Is everything perfectly clear?"

Thirteen affirmative nods.

"Well, then. You four"—he indicated the second-level men—"will serve as general coordinators for the project. The actual intensive work will be carried out by the third-level people, plus you, Spalding."

Kennedy timidly lifted one hand.

"Yes, Theodore?"

"Sir, what about the projects we're currently working on? Are they to be carried on as well?"

Dinoli smiled glacially. "This contract takes precedence over any others we may have signed. Your second-level supervisor will discuss with you the advisability of turning your current project over to a fourth-level man."

"I see," Kennedy said. That was the end of Federated Bauxite, then.

"If everything's understood, men, we can call it a day." Dinoli rose. "We'll work as a tight little unit on this. And we'll prove to the Corporation that they haven't made a mistake in choosing S and D. Won't we, men?"

Thirteen nods.

"Well." The single word was a clearcut dismissal.

They filed out slowly. Kennedy left quietly, deep in what to an observer would have seemed to be thought, but which was actually the opposite—mere mindless intense concentration that allowed him to avoid considering a serious problem of ethics. There was time for that later.

What will Marge say? he wondered. He thought of the simple blank-faced creatures from the film, and of Marge's boundless sympathy for the downtrodden unfortunates of the world. *What will Marge say?* he asked himself worriedly.

3

THE WARM, cheerful, expensive odor of real food filtered through the Kennedy household. Marge bustled about the kitchen, setting the table, while the autochef prepared the meal. They were having shoulder steak, mashed potatoes, garden peas. Nothing on the menu was synthetic; with so many S and D men living clustered in this one Connecticut township, Kennedy could never allow himself the risk of having someone discover he used synthetics. Personally he saw little difference in taste, and an enormous one in price—but prestige was important too, and had to be considered. Third-level men *never* ate synthetics.

"Supper's almost ready," Marge called. She was a brisk, efficient housekeeper.

Kennedy drained the remainder of his pre-dinner cocktail, scratched the cat behind the ears, and flipped a switch on the master control panel of the sound system, cutting out the three living-room speakers and switching the output to the dining area. The playful flutes of Bach's Second Brandenburg came piping out of the other room, accompanied by Marge's lilting, somewhat off-pitch humming.

Kennedy entered the bathroom and jammed his hands into the handkleen socket. The day's grime peeled away. He caught a glimpse of his face, pale, too thin, wrinkles already beginning to form around the eyes even at thirty-two. He wondered if he had always looked this bad; probably not, he admitted.

The handkleen's gentle purr died away. He shook his hands in the unbreakable drying gesture, pointless but habitual, and crossed over into the dining area. Marge was bringing the plates to the table.

"It's Spalding I don't understand," Kennedy said,

abruptly reopening a conversation of an hour before. "Here he is, a fourth-level man jerked up to third just to work on this project, and he's sour as hell on it."

"Maybe Dave isn't interested in the project."

"Maybe—*huh?* What does *that* have to do with it? Any PR man worth his pay can damn well *get* interested in any sort of project. You think I cared about the good folk of Nebraska when I took on that Bauxite deal?"

"No."

"Exactly. And yet within two weeks," Kennedy said, "I was so wrapped up in that project, so identified with it, that it actually *hurt* to be pulled off it and put onto this. Can you understand that?"

Marge smiled sweetly. "I think I can grasp the general picture. But you say Dave's not anxious to work on the new contract? There must be some good reason for that."

"It's the same reason that keeps him down in fourth-level, when he should be in third." Kennedy attacked his meat fiercely, and after a moment went on. "He doesn't have the right spirit. Talent, yes—but that intangible *extra*, no. And don't think Dinoli doesn't know that. I wouldn't be surprised if Dave was put on this thing just as a test— either he delivers the goods now, with third-level responsibilities, or out he goes."

"I've always thought Dave was too sensitive for PR work," Marge said.

"Implying I'm not a sensitive man?"

She shrugged. "Your potatoes are getting cold, darling. Of course you're sensitive, but in a different way. You know?"

"No. But drop the subject." Kennedy had never appreciated his wife's fondness for Spalding, and regularly tried to avoid the necessity of inviting him to their house.

"I suppose Alf Haugen's wild with enthusiasm over the new contract," Marge said.

"Alf's a company-first man. If they gave him the job of selling humanity on turning cannibal, he'd take it on if they boosted his salary. Naturally he's enthusiastic. He'll do anything Dinoli tells him to do, provided there's a buck in it for him."

Bach ended. The robot arms of the sound system gently lifted the record from the turntable and replaced it with

22

an early Beethoven quartet. Kennedy was old-fashioned that way; he still bought discs, rather than tapes.

"You haven't told me what this contract's about yet, you know," Marge said quietly.

Kennedy paused, fork in hand. "It's classified. Top confidential."

She pouted. "You've done classified work before. Have I ever let it spill?"

"This is different," he said slowly. "This absolutely must not leak. I can't, Marge."

They were both silent for a moment, Kennedy knowing that the real reason why he refused to tell her was not that it was classified—he had never kept secrets from her before—but that she would think the project was ugly and brutal. He had always tried to shield her from brutality, even though he knew in some respects she was tougher and more resilient than he was.

"All right," Marge said. *"Don't* tell me. Marie Haugen will. That blabbermouth can't keep quiet for—"

"Marie won't know. Alf won't tell her." Even as he said it, he knew how foolish the words sounded. The food in his stomach felt as if it were curdling. He shook his head bitterly. "Marge, can't you take a straight *no?"*

"If I have to," she said, sighing. She began to clear away the dishes. Kennedy could tell from the sudden angularity of her motions that she was angry.

He shut his eyes for a moment, thinking, looking for the strength to tell her. They had been married eight years —were married on the evening of his college graduation, in 2036. He held a Bachelor of Communications from Northwestern, and, finishing first in his graduating class, had eagerly accepted the bid to come East and work for Steward and Dinoli as a fifth-level man.

Eight years, and he had worked up to third-level, with second perhaps just a few years away. He had tried to be perfectly frank with Marge on all matters, and she loved and respected him for it. But now . . .

He was damned either way. There'd be a wedge between them if he refused to tell her, and perhaps a wider gulf if he did. He began to sweat.

"Come here, Marge," he said in a hoarse voice. "Sit down. I'll tell you about this new contract."

She sat opposite him, watching him with her clear,

dark-blue eyes that had never needed optical correction of any kind. She looked very grave . . . like a serious eight-year-old, he thought suddenly.

"Well?"

"There's been a space expedition to Ganymede. That's one of the moons of Jupiter, you know. It's almost big enough to be a planet itself. Well, they've found people on Ganymede—intelligent people."

"How wonderful! What are they like? Have you seen pictures yet? Are they—"

"Wait a second," Kennedy said, his voice dull. "They also found radioactive ores there. The place is literally packed with minerals that Earth needs desperately. Only the natives refuse to permit any mining operations whatsoever. Some tribal nonsense, I guess. So the Corporation may have some trouble. If there's armed resistance they may have to ask the U.N. Army to intervene in their behalf. It's a matter of the public good; they're not using their minerals, and our entire economy is based on them. So S and D was called in to handle a publicity campaign. On the surface, you see, it might look pretty nasty—that the Corporation was greedily aggressive, attacking primitive creatures, and so forth. Naturally we can't have that kind of publicity. So here's where we come in, to smooth everything over, to make it clear that it's a matter of simple need, and—"

He stopped suddenly, catching the expression that flew momentarily across Marge's face. And was that the edge of a tear in the corner of her eye?

"You dreamed about this last night," she said in a soft, barely audible voice. "About war. You even dreamed we started it. Funny, I never believed in supernatural things like this. Until now."

"Marge!"

"You said it would be a terrible war. Innocent people slaughtered. Remember?"

"It won't be a war, Marge. They'll just occupy the place. Peacefully. We can't let all those valuable ores just rot away there, you know."

She looked at him strangely. "Suppose they object to this occupation. What then?"

"Why—why, how can they? They're just primitive alien

24

beings. I don't even think they have explosives, let alone atomics."

"Not one of you has a conscience," Marge said. "Except Dave Spalding. He's the only one that seems to be upset by this. None of the rest of you are. You just see bonuses and status increments." Her voice was wild and sharp now. "Alf Haugen's probably planning to trade in his car for a custom model. That's all he thinks of. And you, Ted—do you think at all?"

She rose from the table, broke away from him suddenly, and ran off into the darkened living room. He heard the cat squeal in surprise and come dashing out of the room, complaining vehemently. It was a very old cat, and disliked noise and motion.

Things were getting out of hand, Kennedy decided. He tiptoed into the living room. In the darkness he made out a dim form lying on the couch that converted each night into their bed. Marge was sobbing quietly.

Frowning, Kennedy sat down on the edge of the couch and let his hand lightly caress the firm muscles of her back.

"Marge," he whispered. "Don't carry on this way. It's just a job. That's all—just a job. I'm not going to be killing Ganymedeans. I won't be carrying a gun. No matter what I say or think or do, it's going to happen anyway. Why take it out on me? Why hurt *us?*"

The sobbing stopped. He knew she was staring sightlessly in the darkness, battling within herself. Finally she sat up. "All right, darling. I'm taking this whole thing much too seriously, I guess." She tried to smile.

He leaned over and kissed her. But it was a tense, uncertain kiss. They had not seen the end of this quarrel so soon, he realized unhappily.

It was pretty much of a lame evening. They had tentative plans to visit neighbors down the road, but Marge was puffy-eyed from crying, and Kennedy had fallen into a brooding mood of introversion that made any socializing a dismal prospect for the evening. He phoned and begged off, claiming urgent work that simply had to be done this very evening.

There were some awkward moments while he helped her put away the dinner dishes; twice, his eyes met hers and he flinched. He felt very tired. The Ganymede contract was going to occupy his attentions for more than a year, and it wasn't going to be healthy for their marriage if they spent the next thirteen months bickering over the moral issues involved in his acceptance of the assignment.

He had long been proud of the fact that his wife had a mind of her own. Her independent thinking was one of the things he loved her for. But, he saw now, it could also get somewhat burdensome. *Perhaps if we'd had children,* he speculated. *Maybe she wouldn't be so touchy about Causes and Movements.* But they had never had children, and probably never would.

They listened to music awhile—Kennedy only half-listening to the Boccherini quintet Marge loved so, and the Schubert octet. She was terribly fond of chamber music. Ordinarily, Kennedy was, too—but tonight it all seemed frilly and foolish.

At five to eight he suggested, "Let's watch video, eh, Marge? We haven't done that in ages. Let's watch some comic, the way we used to years ago."

"Anything you like, dear," she said mechanically.

He dimmed the lights and switched the set on. It was a new set, hardly a year old, a forty-eight-inch job Kennedy had had installed in the wall opposite the couch. Again, a social necessity. They hardly watched it, normally.

A vortex of colored light swirled dizzyingly for an instant, and then the screen cleared. They had tuned in at the tail end of some program, and a gay, sprightly commercial was on. Kennedy found the dancing stick-figures offensive. He drew Marge close against him on the couch, but she was stiff and unresponsive.

The program ended. The time-bleep bleeped and a deep voice said, "Eight P.M., Eastern Standard Time. From coast to coast, Levree Radionic Watches keep you on time, *all* the time. No gears, no springs."

Again the screen showed the color vortex. Another voice said, "The program normally scheduled for this hour has been canceled to bring you a special Government information release program."

"Let me change the station," Kennedy said. "This'll just be dull junk. We need something funny tonight."

She grasped his arm tightly. "No. Let's see what this is, first. It may be important."

26

An announcer appeared, white-toothed, neatly tanned, his mustache stained red and meticulously clipped. "Good evening," he said. "This is Don Howell from your network newsroom, bringing you a special program covering the big news story of the day, the year, and possibly the century—the discovery of living intelligent beings on another world of this solar system."

Kennedy stiffened. *Already?* he asked himself. *They're releasing it so soon?*

"We must have missed the news bulletins," Marge said.

". . . was revealed by the President at 4:45 this afternoon, at a special press conference. The news electrified a world long fascinated by the possible existence of life in outer space. Details of the expedition are still coming in. However, it's our privilege to present the first public showing of a special film taken by members of the Ganymede expedition!"

The film was the same one Kennedy had seen in Dinoli's office earlier in the day. This time, though, a slick professional commentary had been dubbed in. The newsbreak, Kennedy thought, was apparently the work of a Dinoli second-level man who'd been preparing it for some days. He thought he recognized Ernie Watsinski's touch in the commentary.

When the film reached the point at which the Ganymedean natives appeared, he heard Marge utter a little gasp. "Why, they're like children!" she said. "Defenseless naked creatures! And these are the beings we're going to make war on?"

"We're just going to occupy their territory," Kennedy said stubbornly. "And probably administer it for them. In the long run they'll be a lot better off for it."

"Unless they don't *want* to be better off," she said. "Or administered."

Kennedy shook his head. The public knew, now; come tomorrow, the behind-the-scenes campaign would begin in the offices of S and D. What shall it profit a man, he wondered bleakly, if he gets promoted to second-level, and loses his own wife in the process?

He pulled her tight against him, and after a few moments of hesitation she turned from the screen to him, with what he hoped was unfaked warmth.

4

THE NEXT DAY was the fourth of May, 2044, and the first day of intensive work on what was rapidly becoming known around S and D as the Ganymede Contract.

The dramatic newsbreak of the night before seemed to be the universal topic of discussion; every telefax sheet, every news commentator, every cab driver, had his own set of opinions on the revelation. Kennedy thought of this time as a kind of primordially formless era, before the shrewd minds of Steward and Dinoli went to work shaping a clear-cut and unified public opinion from the present chaos.

They met in the office of Ernie Watsinski, second-level public-relations man, and, incidentally, Dinoli's son-in-law. Watsinski was a tall, stoop-shouldered man of thirty-eight, weak-eyed, with a dome-like skull sparsely covered with sandy hair. Physically he was easy to overlook. But he had a razor-keen mind and an astonishing capacity for quick decisions. He had made second-level at the age of thirty-one, marrying Dinoli's daughter the following year.

He affected twentieth-century functional by way of office furniture, and as a result his private room looked severely ascetic. He perched on the arm of a lemon-colored desk chair and glanced around the room. All eight of the third-level men were present, and Dave Spalding.

"How many of you saw the big newsbreak last night?" he asked. His voice was thin and high-pitched, but still somehow commanding. "All of you? Fine. That's what we like to see here. I worked that program up myself, you know. With aid from Hubbel and Partridge."

He slouched back in the chair, crossing his long spidery legs. "Your colleagues of the sixth- and seventh-level have

28

been running gallups all morning. We've got some of the early results in. Seems almost everyone saw that spot last night, and the early gallups show tremendous interest focused on this Ganymede thing. Okay. The interest exists; it's our job to channel it. That clear and pellucid?"

Without waiting for any response, he continued. "You've all been relieved of your present assignments. You'll be working directly under me; the other three second-level men will be operating peripherally in the same general area, but the key work on this contract is going to come out of this office. I have this straight from Dinoli. Any questions? Good. Now, let's toss this around for half an hour or so. First thing I want is a suggestion for a broad approach. Kennedy?"

Kennedy had been astonished by the sight of his own arm waving in the air. He recovered quickly and said, "I have an idea or two on our general slant, if that hasn't already been determined."

"It hasn't. That's what we're here to do. Go on."

"Well," Kennedy said carefully, "My wife and I saw the program last night. Her reaction to the sight of the Ganymedeans was one of pity. They aroused her maternal protective instincts. I'd suggest we play to this, Ernie. The poor, childlike, innocent Ganymedeans who have to be taken over by our occupation forces for their own good."

"Shrewd point, Kennedy. Let's kick that around a little. Haugen?"

"I'm dead opposed," Haugen said thickly. He twined his fleshy fingers together. "My wife reacted pretty much the same way Kennedy's did. She even thought they were *cute*. The gallups will probably tell you that it was a universal reaction. Okay. We follow Kennedy's plan and build the Ganymedeans up as babes in the woods. What happens if they decide to fight back? Suppose there's a massacre bloodier than all get-out when we try to occupy Ganymede?"

"Amplify," Watsinski said.

"What I'm getting at is this: it may be necessary to gun those creatures down by droves. We can't hide that completely from the public, Ernie. And the outcry will be fantastic. We may even have a revolution on our hands. The government's certainly going to be in trouble."

Watsinski narrowed his eyes until they were mere slits,

and stroked the side of his long, curved nose. At length he said, "Kennedy, you see the flaw in your proposition?"

Shamefaced, Kennedy nodded. Haugen had deflated his idea quickly and sensibly. They would have to prepare the public for the worst.

Watsinski glanced around the table. "Before we move on, is there anyone else who wants to argue for Kennedy's point? I want to make sure."

Slowly Dave Spalding raised his hand. "I do. I think it's wrong to go into this expecting a bloody massacre. The occupation ought to be as peaceful as possible, and if we build up a publicity blanket of love for the Ganymedeans then it damn well *better* be peaceful."

There was an instant of silence. Kennedy distinctly heard Watsinski's sobbing intake of breath, as if he were being very patient. Watsinski said, "Spalding, you're only a fourth-level man, and we can make allowances. But we try to shape public opinion here. We *don't* try to shape the doings of the Corporation to fit the kind of atmosphere we've created. They happen to employ us. This kind of thing has hurt you before, Spalding, and it's likely to hurt you again if you don't get your thinking clarified."

Kennedy glanced quickly down the table at Spalding, and glanced away. The young fourth-level man had gone very pale at the rebuke. His nostrils flickered in momentary anger; he said nothing.

Watsinski said, "Well. We can go ahead, then. Kick it around some more, fellows. I'm listening."

Lloyd Presslie got the floor. "We could take the opposite track. Paint the Ganymedeans as monsters. Alien demons from an ice-bound planet. Wipe this damn motherlove out of the picture, just in case we have to come down on them hard."

Watsinski was smiling, showing yellowish, uneven teeth. "I like," he said gently. "I like. Let's kick it around some more, shall we?"

But Kennedy knew that any further talk was going to be superfluous. Watsinski's smile meant that the meeting had arrived at what was going to be the policy; that Presslie had accidentally hit on the plan which Dinoli and his top staff men had already formulated, and which Watsinski had been prepared to shove down the third-level men's throats, if necessary.

30

Kennedy ate lunch that day, as he had every day of his eight-year employment at Steward and Dinoli, in the agency cafeteria on Floor Ten. He twitchèd his yellow status-card from the protective folder in his wallet, slapped it against the translucent plastic plate in the dispensary wall, and waited for it to be scanned.

A moment later the standard Thursday third-level lunch issued from a slot further down in the dispensary. Kennedy repocketed his meal-ticket and picked up his tray. Algae steak, synthetic vegemix, a cup of pale but undeniably real coffee. Dinoli had never been very liberal with his lunches. The second-level men ate in their private offices, so Kennedy had no idea of what they were served, but he was willing to wager the menu wasn't one hundred percent natural foods.

Just as he started to head for the third-level table in the front of the cafeteria, someone nudged his elbow, nearly spilling his tray. He turned, annoyed.

Dave Spalding stood behind him, smiling apologetically.

"Sorry, Ted. I didn't mean to knock your tray over. But I called you, and you didn't answer."

Kennedy glanced at the tray Spalding held. The fourth-level menu was something he had already thankfully forgotten, and he was not happy to see it again. Weak soup, chlorella patties, protein sauce. Synthetic caffeine drink. He looked away, embarrassed.

"What is it, Dave? You want to talk to me?"

Spalding nodded. "Unless you've already made plans for lunch. We can take one of the tables at the side."

Shrugging, Kennedy agreed. Perhaps Spalding wanted to ask his advice. As a third-level man, it was his responsibility to help any lower-rated man who sought him out.

There were a few small tables arranged at the far side of the cafeteria for meetings such as this. Ordinarily, one ate with one's own level, but tables were provided to care for inter-level lunches as well. It simply would not have done for Kennedy to have had to eat at the fourth-level table in order to speak with Spalding.

They sat down. Kennedy was happy the second-level men ate elsewhere; he did not want his name linked too tightly to Spalding's in Watsinski's mind.

"Can I speak to you with absolute honesty?" Spalding asked.

31

"Of course, Dave." Kennedy felt ill at ease. Spalding, at twenty-eight, was Marge's age—four years his junior. When Harris had left the Agency for independent press-agenting work a year ago, Spalding should have entered third-level. But instead, Lloyd Presslie had been jumped over him into third. "What's on your mind?" Kennedy asked.

Spalding paused, a forkful of chlorella patty poised midway between plate and mouth. "The Ganymede contract. I want to know how you feel about it."

"A job," Kennedy said. "Possibly quite a challenging one."

Spalding's dark eyes seemed to bore into him. He was scowling. "Just a job? A challenge?"

"Should it be anything else?"

"It's the biggest sell since the days of Judas, and you know it as—as *pellucidly* as I do," Spalding said, bitterly mocking Ernie Watsinski's favorite word. "The whole thing is simply a naked grab of strategic territory. And we're supposed to peddle the idea to the public."

"Does it matter," Kennedy asked, "which particular commodity we're selling? If you want to start drawing ethical boundaries, you'd have to ring the whole agency. I've had plenty of jobs just as—well, shady—as this one. So have you. That Federated Bauxite thing I was on, just to take one example—"

"So you had to convince some people in Nebraska that they weren't having their water supply polluted. I suppose that's small enough so you can swallow it down. But Ganymede's too big. We're selling two worlds—ours and theirs. Ted, I want out."

"Out of the contract?"

"Out of the agency," Spalding said.

Kennedy chewed quietly for a moment. "Why are you telling me all this?" he asked after a while.

"I have to tell someone, Ted. And I feel I can trust you. I think you're basically on my side. I know Marge is. She can convince you."

"Keep Marge out of this discussion," Kennedy said, forcing back his anger. Spalding was only a wild-eyed kid, despite his twenty-eight years. Some of them never grew up, never learned that life was essentially a lot of compro-

32

mises within compromises, and you had to do the best you could. "You'd really leave the agency over this contract?"

Spalding looked so pale as to seem ill. "I've been building up to it a long time. We've been handed one sell after another, but this one's too big. It's lousy, Ted. I tried to play along with all the others. But they had to go and yank me out of fourth-level to work on this one. Why?"

"Maybe they wanted to see how you'd react."

"Well, they're going to see," Spalding snapped. "I tried to put in my pitch when we met with Watsinski this morning. It was your point I was defending, too, even if you gave up. But you saw how I got slapped down. Policy on this was set a long time ago, Ted."

Kennedy felt inwardly calm. He mopped up his plate with exaggerated care, thinking that this was no problem of his, that he took a mere intellectual interest in Spalding's qualms of conscience, with no emotional involvement. "You haven't thought this through, Dave. Where would you go? You're not a youngster any more. You're twenty-eight, and still fourth-level. Dinoli's sure to blacklist you. You couldn't get a job anywhere in PR or advertising."

"I wouldn't want one. It would be foolish to jump out of Dinoli into some other place just the same, only not quite as big."

"You couldn't get a job anywhere else, either. Dinoli has influence. And he doesn't like three-year men to quit," Kennedy said.

"You don't understand. I wouldn't get a job. I've always wanted to be a writer, Ted. This is my chance."

"Video? Dinoli has his fingers in that, too. He'll—"

"No. Not video. *Books*, Ted."

For the first time Kennedy realized the glow in Spalding's eyes was as much that of fanaticism as youth. "Books? You can't make a living doing books," Kennedy said. "Could you get along on two or three thousand a year? That's if you're a smash success right away, I mean."

Spalding shrugged. "I'd manage if I had to."

"Don't you want to get married? Isn't there anyone you love, man?"

"There's a girl I love," Spalding said quietly. "But she can wait. She's waited long enough already."

Kennedy studied the younger man's slim, curiously intense face. "Have you mentioned this quitting business to anyone else in the agency yet?"

Spalding shook his head. "I was hoping something might come out of that conference this morning. But nothing did."

"Listen, Dave. Stay here awhile. A week, two, maybe a month. Don't rush into anything." Kennedy wondered why he was going to all this trouble persuading Spalding to stay in a place he obviously hated and was ill-qualified for. "Think about this move for a while. Once you quit Dinoli, you're sunk for good."

Spalding's eyelids drooped broodingly. After a long silence he said, "Maybe you have something there. I'll stick for two weeks more. Just to see if I can bend this contract into a better direction, though. If nothing works out, I'm leaving."

"That's a sensible attitude, kid." The patronizing *kid* annoyed Kennedy as soon as it escaped his mouth, but by then it was too late.

Spalding grinned. "And you're an agency man for life, I suppose? Solidly sold on the virtues of Lou Dinoli?"

"He's no saint," Kennedy said. "Neither am I. It doesn't pay to aim for sainthood these days. But I'll keep my job. And I'll be able to live with my conscience afterward."

"I wonder about that," Spalding murmured.

"What's that?"

"Nothing," Spalding said quickly. "Just shooting my mouth off again. It's an old habit of mine." He grinned pleasantly and said, "Thanks for sparing the time, Ted. You've cleared my mind tremendously. I really appreciate it."

The gong sounded, ending lunch hour. Spalding touched Kennedy's arm in a gesture of gratitude and scampered away, dumping his empty tray in the big hopper.

More slowly, Kennedy followed him, and abstractedly let the plastic tray slide down into the washer's maw. *I have no illusions,* he told himself firmly. *I'm not a fanatic agency man like Haugen. I think some of the things we do are rotten. I think this contract's rotten. But there just isn't any percentage in standing up and saying so. The guy who stands up only gets slapped down twice as hard and twice as fast.*

34

He felt a sudden deep surge of pity for Dave Spalding. You had to pity a man whose conscience wouldn't let him rest. This was no world for a man with a conscience, Kennedy thought morbidly, as he headed back toward his desk to begin sketching out the Ganymede campaign.

5

MAY MOVED ALONG through its second week, and the Steward and Dinoli organization effortlessly made the transition from its previous batch of contracts to the one all-encompassing job they were now committed to. A bright-eyed fourth-level kid named Furman relieved Kennedy of the Federated Bauxite portfolio, and from that moment on he was a full-time member of the Ganymede project.

Watsinski was his immediate superior—the idea-coordinator of the project. Each of the other three second-level men had his own special responsibility in the affair—Kauderer handling space purchasing; McDermott, governmental liaison and United Nations lobbying; Poggioli, opinion sampling and trend-testing. But these were essentially subsidiary enterprises; the central ideological flow was channeled through Watsinski, Dinoli's heir apparent and the reigning boss of the second-level men. Watsinski's team consisted of nine: Kennedy, Haugen, Spalding, Presslie, Cameron, Richardson, Fleischman, Lund, and Whitman. These were the men who would sell Ganymede to the people of Earth.

No one, not even Watsinski, seemed in any great hurry to get the project rolling. They spent the first few days just doodling ideas and filing them without even bringing them up for discussion. It was a curiously low-pressure beginning for a Steward and Dinoli project.

There were several target dates to be kept in mind. Kennedy scribbled them all carefully in his personal notebook as soon as they filtered down from above.

May 21, 2044—*first big publicity push*

July 8—*beginning of transition in public feeling; prepare for unsympathetic depiction of Ganymedeans*

September 17—*intensification of program; building toward climax of operation*

September 22—*Corporation will begin to ask U.N. to consider giving it aid in case necessary; underscore through S and D*

October 11—*Climactic incident will send Corporation before U.N. with a plea for help*

October 17 (optimum desired time)—*United Nations decision to occupy Ganymede to safeguard the rights of Corporation*

Kennedy refrained from letting Marge see the timetable; it was just too neat, too well planned, and he knew what her immediate reaction would be.

It would be pretty much that of Dave Spalding the day the memorandum had been sent around. Spalding's desk had been moved out of the fourth-level quarters, and now he worked near Haugen and Kennedy. He looked up when the sealed envelope was deposited on the corner of his desk, ripped it open, skimmed through it.

"Well, here it is. The blueprint for conquest."

Alf Haugen dropped his memorandum to the shining surface of his desk and glanced at Spalding, a troubled look on his heavy face.

"What the hell do you mean by that?"

Trouble bristled a moment in the office; smoothly Kennedy said, "Always the cynic, eh, Dave? You'd think the Ganymedeans were going to get trampled into the dust."

"Well, we—"

"You have to hand it to Dinoli," Kennedy continued. "He can work out a timetable six months in advance and judge every trend so well we don't need to amend the schedule as much as twenty-four hours."

"It's a trick of the trade," Haugen said. "Dinoli's a shark. A real shark. God damn, but I respect that man! And I don't even care whether he's listening or not!"

"You really think the third-level office is wired?" Spalding asked anxiously.

Haugen shrugged amiably. "Probably is. Dinoli likes to have a loyal staff around him. There are ways of finding out who's loyal. But I don't care. Hell, *I'm* loyal; if old Lou wants to tune in on what I'm saying, I've got nothing to worry about."

Kennedy folded the memorandum and tucked it away; then he left his desk and crossed the floor to Spalding's. Leaning down with both hands on the other's desk, he put his face close to Spalding's and said, "Dave, do you have a free minute? I'm going to Library Deck for a pickup and I need a hand carrying the stuff."

"Why don't you ring for a porter?"

The tip of Spalding's shoe protruded from under his desk. Kennedy found it with his own foot and pressed down hard. "I don't trust those boys. I'd like you to help me out."

Spalding looked puzzled, but he shrugged and nodded. When they were out of the third-level area and in the corridor, Kennedy gripped him tightly by the arm and said in a low voice, "That 'blueprint for conquest' gag was a little out of place, Dave. It wasn't called for."

"Wasn't it?"

"That's neither here nor there. You're not expected to make anti-agency cracks in the third-level area. If Haugen had reported you he'd have been within his rights."

A cold smile crossed Spalding's face. "Is it against the law to speak out against a nasty business deal?"

"Yes," Kennedy said. "Either you stick with it and keep your mouth shut or you get out. One or the other. What happened to your ambitions of a couple of days ago—becoming a writer, and all that?"

Spalding smiled apologetically. "I decided to swallow my qualms and stick with it."

"That's a sensible move, Dave. I figured you'd outgrow that adolescent mood of rebellion. I'm glad to hear you talk this way."

"The devil with you, Ted. I haven't outgrown anything. I'm sticking here because I need the money. I'm drawing third-level pay now, and that's good cabbage. A few more months of Papa Dinoli's shekels and I'll have enough of a nest egg to quit and do what I want to do. What I *really*

37

want to do." Spalding's eyes glittered. "Fight cynicism with cynicism. It's the only way."

Kennedy blinked. He said nothing.

"Now," Spalding went on. "That library pickup. Is it legit, or did you just cook it up so you could give me a word of advice?"

"I just cooked it up," Kennedy admitted.

"I thought so. Mind if I get back to work, then?"

Spalding smiled and ducked past him. "You louse," Kennedy said quietly to himself, at Spalding's retreating back. "You cold-blooded louse."

Kennedy remained in the hall for a moment; then, realizing he was standing frozen with a stupefied expression on his face, he snapped out of it and walked back to his desk.

It wasn't any secret that Dave Spalding regarded the Ganymede contract with loathing. Kennedy had already written that off to Spalding's fuzzy-minded idealism; idealists always had a way of being fuzzy-minded.

But the sudden sharp revelation just now had shown Kennedy a very unfuzzy-minded Spalding, who was cold-bloodedly extracting enough money from the Ganymede contract to let himself get quit of the whole enterprise. That cast a new light on things, Kennedy thought. He felt a faint quiver of doubt. Somehow he couldn't laugh off Spalding's opinion of the contract any more.

Haugen was at the water cooler as Kennedy returned to the third-level area, and Kennedy joined him. The beefy executive was sipping his drink with obvious enjoyment. Spalding was bent studiously over his notes.

"What time's the meeting?" Kennedy asked.

He knew what time it was. But Haugen said, "Watsinski wants us in his office in half an hour. Got any sharp ideas?"

"A few," Kennedy admitted cautiously. "Couple of notions. Maybe Ernie'll take them. Alf?"

"Hey?"

"Tell me something—straight. What do you think of this whole business about Ganymede?"

As soon as he said it, he knew it was a mistake. Haugen turned, peered at him full-face, frowned in puzzlement. "What do I think—huh? About what?"

38

"The contract. Whether it's right." Kennedy began to sweat. He wished he had kept quiet.

"*Right?* Right?" Haugen repeated incredulously. He shrugged. "Is that what you were worrying about? Caught something from Spalding, maybe?"

"Not exactly. Marge worries a lot. She's socially oriented. She keeps bringing the thing up."

Haugen smiled warmly. He was forty, and knew by now he'd never advance beyond third-level; he was serene in the knowledge that his competence would keep him where he was, and that there was no danger of his slipping back or any chance of his moving forward. "Ted, I'm surprised to hear you talk this way. You've got a fine home, a splendid wife, luxury living. You're a third-level exec. You're pulling down thirty thousand a year plus bonuses, and you're bucking for second-level. You'll get there, too—you've got the stuff. I can tell."

Kennedy felt his face going red. "Soft-soap won't answer my questions, Alf."

"This isn't soft-soap. It's fact, plain hard fact. You have all these things. Lots of people don't. Okay. Now you get called in by Dinoli, and he tells you to let the public think thus-and-so about the planet Ganymede, or moon Ganymede, or whatever the blazes it is. Do you stand around asking yourself if this is right?" Haugen chuckled richly. "The hell you do! For thirty thousand a year, *who cares?*"

Kennedy took a sip of water. "Yeah. Yeah."

"You see?"

Kennedy nodded. "I think so," he said.

Half an hour later Kennedy was at his place around the table in Ernie Watsinski's office, sitting next to Haugen and across the table from Spalding. Watsinski sat perfectly quietly, a lanky uncouth figure draped over a chair, waiting for the group to assemble. Richardson was the last man to arrive; he slipped in quietly, hoping no one would notice his tardiness, and in that moment Watsinski came to life.

"Today, gentlemen, is the eleventh of May," he began, in his thin voice. "It's precisely one week since we last met in this room. It's also—I take it you've all seen the time sheet that was circulated this morning; if you haven't, please raise hands—ah, good. As I say, it's also precisely

39

ten days till the beginning of the public phase of our campaign. A lot of work is going into this project, gentlemen —a hell of a lot of work. If you knew how Joe Kauderer is running around lining up media breaks for us—well, you'll know soon enough, when Joe makes his report to you at the big meeting with Dinoli. But the thing is really moving. Really moving.

"Now I've given you this week to think things out, to look at the big picture and fit yourself into it. You know we at S and D regard public relations work as an artistic creation. You're shaping an esthetic whole. The beauty of a fully-developed opinion pattern is like the beauty of a Mona Lisa or a Rembrandt or a Beethoven symphony. If any of you men don't *feel* this Ganymede thing with all you've got, I'd appreciate it if you'd let me know right here and now, or else later in privacy. This has to be real. It has to be *sincere*, gentlemen."

Watsinski seemed to have worked up genuine passion over his rhapsody. His eyes were glossy with the beginnings of tears. Kennedy glanced over at Spalding, but the young man sat tight-jawed without revealing a bit of the emotion he might have been feeling.

"Okay, gentlemen, let's get to work," Watsinski said suddenly, in an entirely different tone of voice. He had descended from empyreal heights with marvelous rapidity. "At our last meeting we decided on our general pattern of approach—it was Lloyd Presslie's suggestion, since taken up with Dinoli and in essence approved, that we take into account the distinct possibility of strong reaction on Ganymede and therefore build the Ganymedeans up as unsympathetic types. I guess you've all been thinking about ways and means of doing this. Richardson, start talking."

All eyes swiveled to the back of the room. This was Watsinski's way of indicating his displeasure at Richardson's tardiness; there would be no other formal reprimand.

Richardson was a thin-lipped professorial type with a dry, pedantic manner. He ran his hands through his thinning hair and said, "I've been thinking of three or four separate multilevel approaches to this thing, Ernie. But I won't throw them all out on the floor right now. The basic handle is a kiddie-approach. Kiddies and women. Men don't form their own opinions, anyway. I propose that we assault this thing by filtering anti-Ganymede stuff into the kiddie shows and the afternoon women-slanted videocasts. I've drawn up a brief on how to go about it, listing fifteen selected shows and the angle of leverage on each one. Some of the writers are former S and D stablemen. You want to go through the brief now, or file it afterwards?"

Watsinski stirred restlessly. "Better save it for later, Claude. We're still searching for the broad patterns. Detailed implementation comes later." Kennedy could see that the second-level man was inwardly displeased that Richardson had come through; Watsinski liked nothing better than to see a staffman squirm and admit he was unprepared. But if you were third-level you just didn't come unprepared to a meeting with Watsinski.

They went around the table. Haugen had developed a slippery idea for feeding pro-Ganymedean stuff into overseas video shows and newspapers, carefully picking the countries, selecting the ones least in favor in the United States at the moment. Then, via a simple contrast-switch, local opinion could be pyramided on the basic proposition, *If they're for it, we're gonna be agin it!*

Watsinski liked that. Fleischman then offered his ideas: a typically Fleischmanoid product, many-layered and obscure, for grabbing public opinion simultaneously at the college and kindergarten level and letting babes and late adolescents serve as propagandists. Watsinski went for that, too.

Then it was Kennedy's turn. He tugged nervously at his collar and put his unopened briefcase before him on the table.

"I've sketched out a plan that substantially dovetails with the ones we've just heard, Ernie. It can be used alongside any or all of them."

"Let's have it."

"In brief, it's this: we need a straw man, a dummy to set up and kick over. Something to engage local sympathies firmly and finally."

Watsinski was nodding. Kennedy moistened his lips. He said, "At the moment the only human beings on Ganymede are a couple of dozen Corporation spacemen and scientists. I don't think there's a woman or a child on the place. Where's the human interest in that? Where's the pathos when we highlight them against the Ganymedeans?

41

Who gives much of a damn about a bunch of Corporation scientists?

"Now," Kennedy went on, "here's my suggestion. We start disseminating word of a colony of Earthmen on Ganymede. Volunteers. A couple of hundred chosen people, brave self-sacrificing men, women, and children. Naturally there isn't any colony there. The Corporation wouldn't send noncombatants into a militarily unsettled area like Ganymede. But the public doesn't have to know that. If we make the doings of the colony consistent, if we start believing in it ourselves—then the public will believe in it too. And once we've got a firm fisthold on their sympathies, we can do anything with them!"

Kennedy had hardly finished speaking when half a dozen hands were in the air. For an instant he thought they were going to laugh him down, but then he saw the way they all looked, and realized his suggestion had inspired them to new heights.

Presslie got the floor and said, "It's a natural! Why, then we can follow through by having the Ganymedeans *wipe out* this colony. It's a sure bet for engaging sympathy in any sort of necessary police action! Innocent women and children perishing, flames, blood—why, this is the handle we need! Of course I can suggest some modifications, but those can come later."

Watsinski nodded. "Kennedy seems to have hit on a sharp idea. I'm going to suggest it to Dinoli as our basic line of approach, and build all the other plans around it. Good work, Kennedy. Lund, let's hear from you, now. I want to kick this all the way round the table."

6

LATER THAT DAY, two hours after the meeting had broken up, Kennedy was working at his desk when the phone chimed. He snatched it up and heard Watsinski's dry voice say, "Kennedy? Ernie here. Can you come over to my place for a few minutes?"

"Be right there, Ernie."

Watsinski was waiting for him when he came in. The second-level man wore a severely funereal business-suit and a glistening red wig. He smiled perfunctorily and beckoned Kennedy to a seat.

"I took up your suggestion with Dinoli," he said immediately, without preface. "The old man loved it. He thinks it's great. So did Kauderer, McDermott, and Poggioli. We had a quick vote on it just before lunch."

Stiffly Kennedy said, "I'm glad to hear it went over, Ernie."

Watsinski nodded. "It went over. Dinoli spent half of lunch talking to Bullard—he's Mr. Big over at the Corporation, you know. They were mapping out the strategy. Dinoli is using your plan as the core of the whole thing."

Kennedy felt a self-satisfied glow. Dammit, it was good to know your voice counted for something around this place. It was always so easy to think you were just a puppet being pushed around by the top-level men with the same ease that you pushed the vast inchoate public mind around.

"I hit a good one, huh, Ernie?"

"You did." Watsinski leaned back and permitted some warmth to enter his face. "I've always liked you, Ted. I think you've got the stuff for second-level. You know what it takes—dogged persistence plus off-beat ingenuity. That isn't an everyday combination of traits. We've got guys who come up with off-beat ideas—Lund, for instance, or Whitman, or sometimes that kid Spalding. But they don't have the push to implement their notions. And then we get the kind like Haugen, the solid pluggers who never make mistakes but who never come up with anything new or fresh either. Well, we need both types down on third-level. But second-level takes something else. I've got it. So do Poggioli and McDermott and Kauderer. I think you have it too, Ted."

"It's good to hear you say that, Ernie. I know you don't go soaping people up."

Watsinski inclined his red wig forward. "This is strictly off the record, Ted. But Frank Poggioli is talking about pulling out of S and D and taking a big network job in video. I know he and Dinoli hashed it out, and Dinoli's willing to let him go."

"The Chief always likes to have his graduates high up in the networks," Kennedy said.

"Sure. Well, in case Poggioli goes, someone'll have to be kicked up to second-level to fill the vacancy. Dinoli also took that up with me this morning. It's between Haugen and Presslie and you. But Presslie's fresh out of fourth-level and I know McDermott's afraid to move anybody up too fast; and they think Haugen's too stodgy. I'm putting my support back of you. That business this morning helped me make up my mind."

"Thanks, Ernie. Thanks." Kennedy wondered why Watsinski was bothering to tell him all this.

Watsinski let his eyes droop quietly closed, and when he opened them again they seemed to be veiled. "Okay. Enough if-talk, Ted. I just wanted you to know where you stand in the agency. I hate to see a man feel insecure when he's in a good position." Watsinski frowned. "You know, there are guys in this agency who don't have the right spirit, and I wish we could root them the hell out of here. Guys who aren't loyal. Guys who don't have the right ideas. Guys whose minds are full of cockeyed garbage served up by antisocial creeps. You know these guys better than I do; you see them through clearer focus. As a prospective second-level man you ought to start thinking about these guys and how we can weed them out. You ought to let me know if you spot any thinking of a negative type. Okay, Ted?"

Kennedy felt a sudden chill. *So that's what he wants*, he thought. *He wants me to spy for him and finger the Spaldings who have qualms about the contract.*

"I guess I see what you mean, Ernie. Well, I'll think about it."

"Sure. Don't rush it or you'll crush it. But I know definitely there are some antisocial elements on our team, and I want to clean them out. So does Dinoli."

The office phone chimed. Watsinski picked it up, listened for a long moment, finally said, "He's here right now, Lou. I'm filling him in. Okay, Chief."

He hung up.

"That was Dinoli. Well, let me get to the main pitch, Ted: we're using the plan you threw out this morning.

44

We're going to invent a colony on Ganymede and in October we're going to have the Ganymedeans launch a savage attack on that colony, and then the Corporation will ask the U.N. to step in and save it. Dinoli wants you to be in charge of developing material on this colony. You'll have sole charge. In essence you'll be doing second-level work. You can name your own staff; pick out anybody you like from third- or fourth-level as your assistant."

"Right now?"

"It would help," Watsinki said.

Kennedy was silent a moment. He pulled a cigarette from an ignitopak, waited for it to glow into life, and with calm deliberation sucked smoke into his lungs. He thought about Watsinski's proposition.

They were setting him up in a big way. On the surface, it was a heartwarming vote of confidence in his abilities—but Kennedy knew enough about the workings of Steward and Dinoli to realize that the upper levels never operated merely on the surface alone. They always played a deep game.

They were putting him into a big post in exchange for something—information, no doubt. They knew the Ganymede contract was a hot item, and they wanted to avoid any leaks by weeding out possible defectors like Spalding. Possibly they had their eye on Spalding already and were simply waiting for Kennedy to confirm their suspicions.

Well, Kennedy thought, *I won't play their game.*

He thought about possible assistants for a moment more. Haugen, Lund, Whitman—

No. There was one man qualified uniquely for the job. One man who would much rather be writing books than handling the Ganymede contract.

Kennedy stared bluntly at Watsinski's thin, shrewd face. "Okay. I've picked my man."

"Who?"

"Dave Spalding," Kennedy said.

For just a fraction of a second Watsinski looked as if Kennedy had kicked him in the teeth. Then control reasserted itself and Watsinski said, in a mellow, even tone, "Okay, Ted, I'll see what I can do to expedite your request. That'll be all for now. Keep up the good work."

That night when Marge asked him how things had gone

during the day, he said shortly, "Pretty fair. Watsinski called me in and said I have a good shot at second-level. They gave me some special work to do."

She was wearing a translucent skylon dress with peekaboo front. As she poured him his drink she said, "I guess you don't want to talk about what you'll be doing."

"I'd rather not, Marge."

"I won't push, dear." She dropped a pale white onion into the cocktail, kissed him, and handed him the drink. He took it and said, "Dave Spalding's going to be working directly with me. And we're actually going to be handling the core of the whole project."

It seemed for a moment that Marge looked surprised. Then she said, "I hope you and Dave will get along better now. It would be too bad if you couldn't cooperate on your work."

Kennedy smiled. "I think we will. I picked him as my assistant myself." He took a deep sip of the drink and got it out of the way just in time as the cat bounded into his lap and curled himself up.

He felt relaxed and happy. This was the way life ought to be: a good job, a good drink, good music playing, your good wife fixing a good supper inside. And after supper some good company, an evening of relaxation, and then a good night in bed. He closed his eyes, listening to the jubilant trumpets of the Purcell Ode on the sound system, and stroked the cat gently with his free hand.

Spalding had taken the news pretty well, he thought. Kennedy had met with him at 2:00 o'clock, shortly after confirmation of the new arrangement had come through from Watsinski, and Spalding had seemed interested and almost enthusiastic about the fictional Ganymedean colony they were about to create. There had been no coldness between them, no raising of knotty moral issues, for which Kennedy was thankful in the extreme.

Instead, Spalding had immediately begun producing a wealth of ideas, characters, incidents, jumping at the work with boyish vigor. Kennedy realized that the four years was a considerable gap; Spalding was still just a kid. He hadn't had time to learn the poised manners of a mature individual. But it would be good for both of them to work together on this project.

Kennedy himself felt a sudden welling of enthusiastic

46

interest. He knew what Watsinski had been talking about when he referred to the esthetic nature of public relations work. It could be a work of art. He and Spalding would give life to a colony of people, endow them with talents and hopes and strivings, interest the people of the world in their hardships and privations and courage.

The music swelled to a climax. Kennedy thought of old Purcell, back there in seventeenth-century England, hearing this glorious music inside his head and painstakingly jotting it onto a sheet of grimy paper—and then of the artists who performed it, the engineers who recorded it, the whole host of participants in the esthetic act. There it was, he thought: an artistic creation. Something that hadn't existed the morning before Purcell inked in his first clef, and something that now belonged to the world.

It was almost the same way with this Ganymede colony he and Spalding would design. Men and women would be able to enter into the life of that colony just as he entered into the life of the musical composition being played. It was almost in a mood of exaltation that Kennedy walked into the dining room at Marge's call.

She smiled at him. "I must have made that cocktail too strong," she said.

"Three-and-a-half to one, or I'm no judge of proportions. Wasn't it?"

"I thought so—but you look so different! Warm and relaxed, Ted."

"And therefore I must be drunk. Because I couldn't possibly be happy and relaxed when I'm sober. Well, I hate to disappoint you, Marge, but I *am* sober. And happy."

"Of course you are, darling. I—"

"And the reason I'm happy," Kennedy continued inexorably, "is only partly because Watsinski said I stood a good chance of making second-level when Poggioli pulls out. That's a minor thing. I'm happy because I have a chance to participate in something real and vital and exciting, and Dave along with me. You know what I'll be doing?"

She smiled. "I didn't want to ask. You're usually so touchy about your work when I ask things."

"Well, I'll tell you." The glow he felt was even stronger.

"Dave and I are going to invent a colony on Ganymede, with people and everything."

He went on to explain in detail what the colony would be like, how he had come to think of the idea, how Watsinski and the others had reacted when he put it forth. He concluded by letting her in on what was really classified material: he told her of Presslie's concluding suggestion, that the colony would be "destroyed" to serve as provocation for the intended United Nations occupation.

"There," he finished. "Isn't that neat? Complete, well rounded, carefully built up. It—"

He stopped. The glow of happiness winked out in an instant. Marge was staring at him with an expression that he could only interpret as one of horror.

"You're serious about this, aren't you?" she asked.

"Of course I am. What's wrong?"

"This whole terrible charade—this fake slush— being used to grab the sympathies of the world. What a gigantic, grisly hoax! And you're *proud* of it!"

"Marge, I—"

"You what?" she asked quietly. "You were sitting there *radiating* content and happiness. How could you?"

"Just take it on its own terms," he said tightly. "As a creative effort. Don't drag moral confusions into it. You always have to cobweb things up by dragging in morality and preachery."

"You *can't* take anything on its own terms, Ted. That's your mistake. You have to look at it in context, and in context I can only say that this thing stinks from top to bottom inside and out."

He slammed his fork to the table. *"Marge!"*

She stared steadily at him. "I guess I spoke out of line, Ted. I'm sorry, darling. I didn't mean to preach." The muscles of her jaws were tightening in convulsive little clumps, and Kennedy saw she was fighting hard to keep back another big emotional outburst. He reached out and gripped her hand.

"Don't get worked up over this thing," he told her. "From now on let me leave my job at 2:30 and forget it until the next morning. Otherwise we'll be at each other's throats all the time."

"You're right, dear. We'd better do that."

He turned his attention back to his meal. But the food

seemed dead and tasteless now, and he was totally unable to recapture the euphoric mood of just a few moments before.

A vast gulf was opening between himself and his wife, and it was getting wider day by day. He thought back over that glow of contentment and wondered how he could ever have attained it. What he and Spalding would be doing was a pretty soulless enterprise, he admitted to himself. There was nothing nice about it. And yet he had worked himself up into a fine esthetic frenzy over it, until Marge's few harsh words had opened his eyes.

And I was proud of it, he thought. My God, don't I ever *think* at all?

7

JUNE 31, 2044—Leap Year World Holiday, by the Permanent Calendar. The extra day, intercalated in the otherwise changeless calendar every four years to take up the slack of the six hours and some minutes the Permanent Calendar was forced to ignore.

A day of revelry, Kennedy thought. A day between the days, a day that was neither Monday, Tuesday, Wednesday nor Thursday, nor Friday, Saturday or even Sunday. A timeless day on which no one worked except for holiday double-pay, on which even the rules of civilization went into the discard heap for twenty-four hours. It fell between Saturday, June thirtieth and Sunday, July first and since this was a leap year there would be two nameless days instead of the usual one at the end of the year.

The Kennedys chose to spend their day at Joyland Amusement Park on the Floating Island in Long Island Sound. Privately, Kennedy detested the hustle and bustle of the World Holidays; but they were family customs, deeply embedded in his way of life, and he never dared to speak out against them.

The road was crowded. Bumper to bumper, deflector plate to deflector plate, the little enameled beetles clung together on the Thruway. Kennedy sweated behind the wheel. The air-conditioners labored mightily. At his side Marge looked fresh and gay in her light summer clothes, red halter and light blue briefs. Her legs glistened; she wore the newest aluminum sprayons.

"The Egyptians had a better slant on this leap year business," he said. "Every year they saved up the fragment of a day that was left over, and let them pile up in the back room of the temple. Then every one thousand four hundred and sixty years all those quarter-days amounted to one full year, and there they were with a whole year that they didn't figure into the calendars. The Sothic year. Of course, the seasons got pretty loused up while waiting for the Sothic year to come around, but that was okay. They held big festivals all that year. An eagle with painted wings was burned alive in a nest of palm branches to celebrate the event. And then the seasons came right again. Origin of the Phoenix legend."

Marge giggled. Up ahead a car stalled in the furious heat and the radar eye of Kennedy's automatic brake picked up the impulse and throttled the turbos; he and Marge rocked slightly forward as the car slowed to thirty.

"It was a fine system," he went on. "And Egypt lasted long enough to celebrate two or three Sothic years. Emperor Augustus killed the Phoenix in 30 B.C. when he stabilized the Egyptian calendar. No more years of festival. We're lucky to get a day once every four years."

The car's air-conditioners whined sourly as the vehicle came to a complete halt. Marge said, "One thousand four hundred and sixty years ago America belonged to the Indians. Our ancestors were painting themselves blue and worshipping Druids in wicker baskets. And in the same amount of years hence we'll all be forgotten. Sothic years won't work nowadays; by the time the next one comes around nobody'll remember to insert it in the calendar."

"Sure they will. Otherwise you'll have winter coming in May and summer in November and—" The congestion cleared ahead and he whisked the car on. The inside-outside thermometer read sixty-nine inside the car, ninety-seven outside. The compass told him they were heading westward along the Thruway toward the Sound. Not a bad car at all, he thought, my battered old '42 Frontenac. Hardly in the class with Haugen's new Chevvy-Caddy, of course, but ample for my purposes.

They reached another snag in the traffic pattern. Kennedy let go of the wheel and let his hand rest lightly on his wife's cool knee.

"Ted?"

"Eh?"

"Let's try to have a good time together today. Relaxed. Calm. Just having fun."

"Sure, Marge. Today's World Holiday. No ulcers today." He flopped back against the cushion as the car started moving violently. *Damn!* These holiday drivers!"

It had been a rough month. Rough, but exciting. He and Spalding had thrown themselves full force into the pseudo-colony on Ganymede. Endless reams of paper covered with biographical sketches of people who weren't, thick dossiers on Ganymedean weather and the rigors of life in a dome and a million other things. It was like writing a story of space adventure, Kennedy thought, with one minor wrinkle: this wasn't for the fantasy mags. It was going out over the newstapes and the fax sheets and people were gobbling it up.

It went like this:

"Ganymede, 23 May 2044—Another day passed in relative comfort for the Extraterrestrial Development and Exploration Corporation's experimental volunteer station on the tiny world of Ganymede, after the heavy snowfall of yesterday. Lester Brookman, Colony Director, commented, 'Except for the usual hazards of life on an alien world, we're doing fine.'

"The colony's one invalid was reported in good health. She is Mrs. Helene Davenant, thirty-one, wife of an atmospheric engineer, who suffered an appendicitis attack early yesterday morning. Colony Surgeon David Hornsfall operated immediately. Dr. Hornsfall said after the operation, 'Mrs. Davenant is in good shape and there is no danger of complications. The low gravity will aid in her quick recovery and I hope to have her back at work in the hydroponics shed in a few days.' The news eased fears of

51

millions on Earth who were thrown into alarm by a premature report of peritonitis."

And so it went, Kennedy thought. Emotional involvement. Soap opera on a cosmic scale. It was now a little over a month since the Kennedy-Spalding pseudo-colony had received its official unveiling, and in that month life with Marge had grown increasingly difficult.

It was nothing overt, of course. She never spoke of Kennedy's work. But there were the silences in the evening where once there had been enthusiastic chatter, the slight stiffness of the jaws and lips, the faint aloofness. They were not close any more, and even their banter had a strained, artificial character.

Well, he thought, maybe she'd get over it. Dinoli and Watsinski and the others were excited about the things he was doing with the project; he was making big strides upward in the agency, and that had to be taken into account. And today being a holiday, he hoped he might be able to effect some sort of rapprochement between Marge and himself. He banked the car sharply and sent it rocketing up the arching ramp that took it to the Joyland Bridge.

Joyland covered forty sprawling acres on the Floating Island in the Sound—built at the turn of the century for the Peace Fair of 2000–2001. The island did not float now, of course; it was solidly anchored to the floor of the Sound. Once it had floated, though, at the time of the Fair, and the only way to get there was to take a ferry that would chase the island as it moved rapidly around the Sound on its peregrinations. But the upkeep of the giant engines that powered the island had been too great; thirty years ago they had been ripped out and the island anchored a mile off shore, but the old name still clung.

The bridge to the island was a shimmering thread painfully bright in the noonday sun. Kennedy paused at the toll bridge and watched the hundreds of cars creeping one after the other across the span. The under-level of the bridge was empty; by nightfall it would be packed with returning cars. He dropped his dollar in the tollkeep's hands and spurred the car ahead, onto the bridge.

Crossing took fifteen minutes; parking the car, another fifteen. Finally he was free of routine, with a parking check in his pocket and a fun-hat on his head. Marge wore one too: a huge orange thing with myriad quivering paper snakes that gave her a Medusa-like appearance. His was more somber, a black and gray mortician's topper. Elsewhere he saw Roman helmets and horned Viking domes. The place was crowded with fun-seekers in various degrees of nudity; custom prevented any indecencies, but in their attempts to evade the heat most people had stripped down to a minimum, except for those few bundled-up unfortunates who still feared overexposure to the sun.

A girl in her twenties wandered by, hatless, disheveled, wearing only a pair of briefs; she clutched her halter in one hand, a drink flask in the other. Marge pointed to her and Kennedy nodded. She started to reel forward; a moment later she would have fallen and perhaps been trampled underfoot, but a smiling guard in Joyland's green uniform appeared from nowhere to catch her and gently drag her away into the shade. *This is World Holiday,* Kennedy thought. *When we step outside ourselves and leave our ulcers home.*

"Where do we begin?" Marge asked. It was the old problem: there was much to see, so many things to do. A gleaming sign advertised the next firing of the big rocket. There was a barren area on the west shore of the island where passenger rockets were fired; they traveled sixty or seventy miles up, gave the passengers a good squint at the spinning orb of Earth, and plunged back down to make a neat landing on the field. There hadn't been a major accident since 2039, when a hundred people died through a slight miscalculation and cast a shadow over a gay Sunday afternoon. Price was ten dollars a head, but Kennedy had no desire to ride the rocket.

Elsewhere there were roller coasters, drink parlors, fun houses, side shows, a swimming pool, a waxworks. One building in the center of the gaming area specialized in a more private sort of fun; for three dollars a pleasure-seeker and his companion could rent a small air-conditioned room with a bed for an hour. For three dollars more, a girl could sometimes be supplied. This was World Holiday, and fun was unlimited.

They bought tickets for the roller coaster and strapped themselves in tight. The car was jet-powered; it took off with a lurching thrust and kept going down the track, up and around, nightmarishly twisting and plunging. There

53

was always the added uncertainty of catching up with the car before yours; there was a shield, but it wasn't very substantial, and you might just get a jet-blast from the preceding car. It didn't happen often, of course.

At the end of the ride, dizzy, exhausted, they clung to each other and laughed. Arm in arm, they staggered across to a drink parlor and ordered double Scotches at the outside window. In the dimness within, Kennedy saw a man in his fifties plunging wildly around in an alcoholic dance; he leaped up in a final frenzy, started to fall toward the floor, and an ever-present Joyland guard appeared and scooped him up in mid-fall. Kennedy sipped his drink and smiled at Marge. She smiled back with what seemed like sincere warmth. He wondered.

They headed down the main concourse, past the cheap booths that in other years they had always ignored. But this time Marge stopped and tugged at his arm.

"Look at that one!"

"Come on, Marge—you know these things are all rigged. I want to go to the fun house."

"No—hold it, Ted. Look."

He looked. There was a new booth, one that he had never seen before. The flashy sign winked at them: *Send A Letter To Ganymede.*

A toothy, bare-chested carny man leaned forward over the counter, smiling jovially and inviting trade. Next to him a woman in yellow briefs and bandeau frowned in concentration as she filled out what seemed to be a telegram form.

"Come on, friends! Send your best wishes to the brave folks on Ganymede! Only one dollar for a ten-word message! Let them know how you feel about their valiant work!"

"See it, Ted?"

Kennedy nodded. "Let's go over. I want to find out a few things."

The carny man grinned at them. "Care to send a letter to Ganymede, friends? Only a dollar." He shoved a yellow blank and a pencil at them.

The woman finished her message and handed it back. Kennedy caught only the heading at the top. It was addressed to Mrs. Helen Davenant, the appendicitis victim. A get-well message, he thought.

Quietly he said, "This is a new booth, isn't it?"

"The newest in the place! Just put it up last week. And doing very well, too. Would you like——"

"Just a minute," Kennedy said. "Whose idea was it? Do you know a Mr. Watsinski? Or Poggioli?"

"What are you, a detective? Come on, there are people waiting. Step right up, friends! Don't go away, lady—the brave pioneers on Ganymede want to hear from you!"

At his left a fat, middle-aged woman was writing a letter that began, *Dear Dr. Hornsfall*—

"Let's go, Ted," Marge said suddenly.

"No. Just a second." He yanked a dollar out of his wallet, slapped it down, and picked up a pencil. With quick sloppy strokes he wrote: *Dear Director Brookman, Hope all is well with colony; too bad you're just a publicity man's soap bubble. Sincerely, Jasper Greeblefizz.*

He handed over the filled-in sheet and said, "Here, make sure this gets delivered. Come on away from here, Marge."

As he stepped out onto the main concourse again he heard the booth-tender's raucous voice: "Hey, mister, you got too many words in this message! You only allowed ten words and you got fifteen!"

Kennedy ignored him. He grasped Marge tightly by the hand and walked on at a rapid clip.

"You think my letter will get there?" he asked tightly. "You think Director Brookman will answer it?"

She looked at him strangely. Sweat was running down her face and shoulders. "I don't know why you're so upset, Ted. It's all part of the general picture, isn't it? This is a very clever gimmick."

"Yeah," he said. He looked back and saw a line of people waiting to send letters to the brave pioneers on Ganymede. A very clever gimmick. Very clever.

A woman in her late thirties came running by, face frozen in a horrified smile. She wore bright blue lipstick that was smeared all over her face, and she was clutching her tattered halter together with one hand.

In hot pursuit came a much younger man with the bright fierce eyes of a satyr. He was yelling, "Come back, Libby, we still got half an hour paid for!"

Kennedy smiled crookedly. World Holiday. Step outside yourself and leave your ulcers behind. Girls who were the epitome of prudishness thought nothing of whipping off their halters and letting the breeze cool their breasts until the park police intervened. Sober second-level men could ease their tensions in a frenzied alcoholic jig.

But World Holiday was no holiday for him. There was no escaping Ganymede even out here. He was worse off than the carny men who had to work on World Holiday, he thought; at least they drew double pay.

Marge squeezed his hand. "You look funny. You're all right, aren't you, Ted?"

"Sure. Sure. The heat, that's all. I'd be cooked without this hat."

Somehow he pretended gaiety. They had another drink, and another. They looped the loop and rode the caterpillars and goggled at the sweating freaks in the sideshow, and had more drinks. They met Mike Cameron and his wife; the third-level man looked drunk and so did his blond wife. Jerrie Cameron brushed up against Kennedy in open invitation, but he ignored it. The Camerons reeled on toward the rocket. Kennedy and Marge had another drink.

Sometime later they bought tickets for the swimming pool, the one place in Joyland where nudity went unquestioned, and spent an hour bobbing in the warm, chlorinated water. Toward evening they watched the fireworks display and wandered down to the rocket-field to see the big missile come in for a landing.

Kennedy felt dizzy and when he looked at Marge she was smiling crookedly. They wearily retraced their steps to the exit. The *Send A Letter To Ganymede* booth was doing land-office business. The program was a success, Kennedy realized dimly; even Joyland recognized the impact of his Ganymede colony on the nation.

At the parking lot the attendant was dispensing sober-tabs for all drivers; you couldn't get your car until you took one. Kennedy swallowed the tasteless little pellet and felt his mind clearing. His stomach began to knot again. He paused by his car, watching the purple and aureate brilliance of the fireworks in the dust-hung sky, listening to the big swoosh of the departing rocket.

The fun would go on all night. There was always Sunday for recuperating. But he felt no more desire for amusement, and drove home slowly and cautiously, with his hand grimly gripping the wheel. Marge was exhausted; she curled up into a fetal ball on the back seat and slept. Kennedy wondered about the Camerons, and if Jerrie had found the partner she so obviously was searching for.

Happy World Holiday to me, he thought tiredly. *Happy, happy, happy.*

8

SUNDAY WAS a gloom-shrouded botch of a day. Kennedy slept late, dreaming of the harsh hues of Joyland, and woke with his mind still clouded by bitterness and his head aching. He spent an awkward, uncomfortable day in and around the house with Marge. The 'fax-sheet gave the rundown on the World Holiday damage: a thousand lives lost in the Appalachia district alone, much carnage, property destruction, theft. A good day's fun.

It was his turn to operate the car-pool come Monday, the second of July, as 2044 swung into its second half. When he reached the office he found a crisp little note waiting for him on his desk:

Floor Nine
6:57 A.M.

Ted:
   Would you stop off at my office at 8:30 this morning? We're having an important visitor.
LD:lk
                                        Lou

Curious, he arrived at Dinoli's office a little ahead of time and cooled his heels in the big man's oak-paneled foyer for a while until a white-toothed secretary ushered him through the maze into the first-level suite.

There was quite a turnout in Dinoli's office. Dinoli himself faced the door, keen-eyed and wide awake, hunched over with his gnarled hands locked. Kennedy smiled hello. Standing around Dinoli were four men: Watsinski, looking bored; McDermott, the tough little gamecock of a second-level man who was handling governmental liaison on the Ganymede Contract; Executive Hubbel of the Corporation. There was also a fourth man, thick-necked and coarse-featured, with a broad, genial smile and a delicate network of broken capillaries spread out over his face.

Dinoli said, "Mr. Bullard, I'd like you to meet Theodore Kennedy, Executive Third-Level of Steward and Dinoli."

Bullard swung forward. He was a bull of a man, six four or more in height, with the biggest hands Kennedy had ever seen. He proffered one, mangled Kennedy's hand momentarily in greeting, and boomed, "Very pleased to meet you, Mr. Kennedy. I've heard wonderful things about your work from Mr. Dinoli here."

"Thank you, sir."

Kennedy looked around. Despite himself he felt a little wobbly-kneed; this was *very* big brass. Two first-level men in the same room.

"Did you enjoy your holiday?" Dinoli asked, in his dark vast voice.

"Yes, sir. It was very good, sir."

"Glad to hear it. You know, of course, that Mr. Bullard here is head of the Corporation?"

Kennedy nodded. Bullard swung himself up on the corner of Dinoli's conference table, crossed his long legs, took out an ignitopak and offered Kennedy a cigarette. He took it. To refuse would have been a mortal insult in such a meeting.

Smiling, Bullard said, "I understand you're the man who's responsible for development of the—ah—colony on Ganymede. I want to tell you that it's a brilliant concept. Brilliant."

Kennedy was silent. He was tired of saying, *Thank you, sir.*

Bullard went on. "The whole nation—the whole world —is enraptured by the struggles of the unfortunate souls you've invented. And I understand you and you alone have charge of the project."

"I have an assistant, sir. A man named Spalding. He's been a great help."

58

He saw Watsinski pale; Dinoli seemed to scowl. A little taken aback, Bullard said, "Ah, yes. But the main responsibility is yours. And that's why I've come over here this morning to make this offer to you."

"Offer, sir?"

"A very fine one. You've succeeded in capturing the feel of the Ganymede terrain beautifully, considering the second-hand nature of your data. But Mr. Dinoli and I believe that you'd so an even finer job if you had a little actual experience with living conditions on Ganymede. It would give your project that extra touch of reality that would insure the success of the campaign."

Kennedy blinked. Dinoli was beaming.

Bullard said, "There's a supply ship leaving shortly for the Ganymede outpost. There is room for one passenger aboard that ship. I've spoken to Mr. Dinoli and we've agreed to offer you a chance to be that passenger. You can spend three weeks on Ganymede at Corporation expense. How would you like that?"

Kennedy felt steamrollered. He took a fumbling step backward and grabbed a chair. "Sir, I—"

"You want time to think about it. I understand how it is. You're in the midst of a difficult work program. You have certain personal commitments. Well, the ship departs on Thursday. If you care to be on it, all you need to do is say the word."

Kennedy looked at Dinoli, at Watsinski, at McDermott. Their faces gave no hint of feeling. They wanted him to go. They wanted him to drop everything and race off to a cold little iceball in space and live there for three weeks in utter privation so the campaign could be more realistic.

It was impossible to come right out and say no, right here. He would have to stall. "I'll have to take the matter up with my wife, of course. This is so sudden. This great opportunity—"

"Of course," Bullard said. "Well, notify Mr. Dinoli on Wednesday. He'll contact me and make the final arrangements for transporting you."

Signed, sealed, and delivered, Kennedy thought. "Yes, sir," he said hoarsely. "Thank you, sir." To Dinoli he said: "Is there anything else, Mr. Dinoli?"

"No, Ted. That'll be all. Just wanted to let you know the good news, son."

"Thank you, sir," Kennedy mouthed uncertainly. A secretary showed him out.

He returned numbly to his office on Eleven, the office he now shared with Dave Spalding. Trip to Ganymede, he thought. I'll tell them Marge won't let me go. That we're expecting a baby. Anything.

It wouldn't look good, his refusing. But he was damned if he was going to spend three weeks living under the conditions he'd been writing about.

"You look as if you've been guillotined," Spalding said, as Kennedy came in. "They didn't fire you!"

"No such luck. I've got a great big opportunity. The Corporation's offering me a three-week trip to Ganymede to get the feel of things."

A sudden flicker of eagerness came into Spalding's lean face. It was an ugly look, as if Spalding had realized that *he* would be in charge, doing second-level work, all the time Kennedy was gone. "You're accepting, of course?"

Kennedy grimaced. "If I'm buffaloed into it. But I'm sure Marge will howl. She hates to be left alone even for *one* night. And three weeks—"

"She can't go with you?"

"There's just one passage available. I'd be leaving on Thursday if I accept. But that would leave you in charge of the project, wouldn't it?"

"I can handle it."

"I know you can. But suppose you pick the time I'm gone to have another attack of ethics? Suppose you walk out while I'm up in outer space, and leave the project flat? What's Watsinski going to do—say all communications with Ganymede have been suddenly cut off, and wait for me to get back to patch up the damage?"

Spalding's lips tightened. "I told you I didn't plan any walkouts. I can't afford to quit yet. I haven't shown any signs of it in the last five weeks, have I? I've been working like a dog on this project."

"I'm sorry, Dave. I had a rough weekend. I didn't mean to come down on you like that. Let's get to work."

He pulled down one of the big loose-leaf volumes they had made up. They had written out detailed biographies of each of the three hundred and thirteen colonists with whom they had populated Ganymede, and each morning they picked a different one to feature in the newsbreaks.

"I think it's time to get Mary Walls pregnant," Kennedy said. "We haven't had a pregnancy on Ganymede yet. You have the medical background Rollins dug up?"

Spalding produced a slim portfolio bound in black leather—a doctor's report on possible medical problems in the colony. Childbirth under low gravity, pressure diseases, things like that.

Spalding typed out a press release about the first pregnancy on Ganymede, with quotes from the happy mother-to-be, the stunned prospective father ("Gosh, this is great news! I know my Ma back in Texas will jump up and clack her heels when she finds out about Mary!") and, of course, from the ever-talkative Director Brookman.

While he worked, Kennedy checked the photo file for a snapshot of Mary Walls—agency technicians had prepared a phony composograph of every member of the colony—and readied it for release with Spalding's newsbreak. He added the day's news to the Colony Chronicle he was writing—excerpts were being printed daily in the tabloids—and wrote a note to himself to remember that a maternity outfit would need to be ordered before Thursday for Mrs. Walls, to be shipped up on the next supply ship.

Thought of the supply ship brought him back to his own predicament. *Dammit,* he thought, *I don't want to go to Ganymede!*

It had gotten to the point where he believed in his colony up there. He could picture slab-jawed Director Brookman, an outwardly fierce, inwardly sentimental man, could picture rosy-cheeked Mary Walls being told by mustachioed Dr. Hornsfall that she was going to be blessed with a child—

And it was all phony. The outpost on Ganymede consisted of a couple of dozen foul-smelling bearded spacemen, period. He didn't want to go there.

He realized that Spalding could handle the project perfectly well without him. It was running smoothly, now; the news sources were open and well oiled, the populace was hooked, the three hundred and thirteen colonists had assumed three dimensions not only in his mind but in Spalding's and in the rest of the world's. The colony had a life of its own now. Spalding would merely have to extend its activities day by day in his absence.

They phoned in the pregnancy story before noon, and

got busy sketching out the next day's work. Spalding was writing Director Brookman's autobiography, to be serialized in some big weekly—they were still pondering bids—while Kennedy blocked in succeeding events in Mary Walls' pregnancy. He toyed momentarily with the idea of having her suffer a miscarriage in about two months' time, but rejected it; it would be good for a moment's pathos, but quickly forgotten. Having her stay pregnant would be more effective.

Near closing time the reaction hit him, as it did every day toward the finish. He sat back and stared at his trembling hands.

My God, he thought, *this is the biggest hoax humanity has ever known. And I originated it.*

He estimated that perhaps fifty people were in on the hoax now. That was too many. What if one of them cracked up and spilled it all? Would they all be lynched?

They would not, he answered himself. The thing was too firmly embedded in reality by now. He had done his job too well. If someone—anyone—stood up and yelled that it was all a fake, that there was no colony on Ganymede, it would be a simple matter to laugh it down as crackpottery and go ahead manufacturing the next day's set of press releases.

But still the enormity of it chilled him. He looked at Spalding, busily clacking out copy, and shuddered. By now the afternoon telefax sheets were spewing forth the joyous news that Mary Walls—petite little Mary Walls, twenty-five, red-haired, a colony dietician, married two years to lanky Mike Walls, twenty-nine, of Houston, Texas—was about to bear young.

He clenched his fists. Where did it stop, he wondered? Was anything real?

Was he, he wondered, just part of a fictitious press release dreamed up by some glib public relations man elsewhere? Did Mary Walls, up there on Ganymede, know that she was a cardboard figure being manipulated by a harrowed-looking man in New York, that her pregnancy had been brought about not by her loving husband's caress but by a divine gesture on the part of one Theodore Kennedy?

He wiped away sweat. A heavy fist thundered on their

glassite cubicle and he looked up to see Alf Haugen grinning at him.

"Come on, geniuses. It's closing time and I want to get out of here!"

They locked away their books and the car-pool people assembled. Kennedy dropped them each off at their destinations, and finally swung his car into his own garage.

Marge had his afternoon cocktail ready for him. He told her about Bullard's visit, about Dinoli's offer. "So they want to send me to Ganymede for three weeks, and I'd be leaving Thursday? How d'you like that!"

She smiled. "I think it's wonderful! I'll miss you, of course, but—"

His mouth sagged open. "You think I'm going to accept this crazy deal?"

"Aren't you?"

"But I thought—" He closed his eyes a moment. "You *want* me to go, Marge?"

"It's a grand opportunity for you, dear. You may never get another chance to see space. And it's safe, isn't it? They say space travel is safer than riding in a car." She laughed. It was a brittle laugh that told Kennedy a great many things he did not want to know.

She wants me to go, he thought. *She wants to get rid of me for three weeks.*

He took a deep, calm sip. "As a matter of fact, I have until Wednesday to make up my mind," he said. "I told them I'd have to discuss the matter with you before I could agree to anything. But I guess it's okay with you."

Her voice cracked a little as she said, "I certainly wouldn't object. Have I ever stood in the way of your advancement, Ted?"

9

THE SHIP left at 1100 sharp on Thursday, July 5, 2044, and Ted Kennedy was aboard it.

The departure went smoothly and on schedule. The ship

63

was nameless, bearing only the number GC-1073; the captain was a gruff man named Hills who did not seem pleased at the prospect of ferrying a groundlubber along with him to Ganymede. Blast-off was held at Spacefield Seven, a wide jet-blasted area in the flatlands of New Jersey that served as the sole spaceport for the eastern half of the United States.

A small group of friends and well-wishers rode out with Kennedy in the jetcab to see him off. Marge came, and Dave Spalding, and Mike Cameron, and Ernie Watsinski. Kennedy sat moodily in the corner of the cab, staring downward at the smoke-stained sky of industrialized New Jersey, saying nothing, thinking dark thoughts.

He was not looking forward to the trip at all.

Space travel, to him, was still something new and risky. There had been plenty of flights; space travel was forty years old and far from being in the pioneering stage. There had been flights to Mars and Venus, and there was a thriving colony of engineers living in a dome on Luna. Captain Hills had made the Ganymede run a dozen times in the past year. But still Kennedy was nervous.

He was being railroaded. They were all conspiring, he thought, all the smiling false friends who gathered around him. They wanted to send him off to the airless ball of ice halfway across the sky.

The ship was a thin needle standing on its tail, very much alone in the middle of the vast, grassless field. Little trucks had rolled up around it; one was feeding fuel into the reaction-mass hold, one was laden down with supplies for the men of the outpost, another carried mail—*real* mail, not the carnival-inspired fakery Kennedy had seen on World Holiday—for the men up there.

The ship would carry a crew of six, plus cargo. The invoices listed Kennedy as part of the cargo.

He stood nervously at the edge of the field, watching the ship being loaded and half-listening to the chatter of his farewell committee. A tall gaunt-looking man in a baggy gray uniform came up to them and without waiting for silence said, "Which one of you is Kennedy?"

"I am." It was almost a croak.

"Glad to know you. I'm Charley Sizer, ship's medic. Come on with me."

Kennedy looked at his watch. "But it's an hour till blastoff time."

Sizer grinned. "Indeed it is. I want to get you loaded up with gravanol so acceleration doesn't catch you by surprise. When that big fist comes down you won't like it. Let's go, now—you're holding up the works."

Kennedy glanced around at the suddenly solemn little group and said, "Well, I guess this is it. See you all three weeks from now. Ernie, make sure my paychecks get sent home on time." He waited a couple of seconds more. "Marge?" he said finally. "Can I get a kiss good-bye?"

"I'm sorry, Ted." She pecked at his lips and stepped back. He grinned lopsidedly and let Sizer lead him away.

He clambered up the catwalk into the ship. It was hardly an appealing interior. The ship was poorly lit and narrow; the companionways were strictly utilitarian. This was no shiny passenger ship. Racks of spacesuits hung to one side; far to the front he saw two men peering at a vastly complex control panel.

"Here's where you'll stay," Sizer said, indicating a sort of hammock swung between two girders. "Suppose you climb in now and I'll let you have the gravanol pill."

Kennedy climbed in. There was a viewplate just to the left of his head, and he glanced out and saw Marge and Watsinski and the others standing far away, at the edge of the field, watching the ship. Sizer bustled efficiently around him, strapping a safety-webbing over him. The gaunt medic vanished and returned a few minutes later with a water flask and a small bluish pill.

"This stuff will take all the fret out of blast-off," Sizer explained. "We could hit ten or fifteen g's and you wouldn't even know it. You'll sleep like a babe." He handed the pill to Kennedy, who swallowed it, finding it tasteless, and gulped water. Kennedy felt no internal changes that would make him resistant to gravity.

He rolled his eyes toward the right. "Say—what happens if there's an accident? I mean, where's my spacesuit? I ought to know where it is, in case—"

Sizer chuckled. "It takes about a month of training to learn how to live inside a spacesuit, brother. There just isn't any sense in giving you one. But there aren't going to be any accidents. Haven't they told you space flight's safer than driving a car?"

"Yes, but—"

"But nothing. The ship's in perfect order. Nothing can go wrong. You've got Newton's laws of physics working on your side all the way from here to Ganymede and back, and no crazy Holiday drivers coming toward you in your own lane. Just lie back and relax. You'll doze off soon. Next thing you know, we'll be past the Moon and Ganymede-bound."

Kennedy started to protest that he wasn't sleepy, that he was much too tense to be able to fall asleep. But even as he started to protest, he felt a wave of fatigue sweep over him. He yawned.

Grinning, Sizer said, "Don't worry, now. See you later, friend." He threaded his way forward.

Kennedy lay back. He was securely webbed down in the acceleration hammock; he could hardly move. Drowsiness was getting him now. He saw his watch dimly and made out the time as 1045. Fifteen minutes to blast-off. Through the port he saw the little trucks rolling away.

Sleep blurred his vision as the time crawled on toward 1100. He wanted to be awake at the moment of blast-off, to feel the impact, to see Earth leap away from them with sudden ferocity. But he was getting tired. *I'll just close my eyes a second,* he thought. *Just catch forty winks or so before we lift.*

He let his eyelids drop.

A few minutes later he heard the sound of chuckling. Someone touched his arm. He blinked his eyes open and saw Medic Sizer and Captain Hills standing next to his hammock, looking intently at him.

"There something wrong?" he asked in alarm.

"We just wanted to find out how you were doing," Hills said. "Everything okay?"

"Couldn't be better. I'm loose and relaxed. But isn't it almost time for blast-off?"

Hills laughed shortly. "Yeh. That's a good one. Look out that port, Mr. Kennedy."

Numbly Kennedy swiveled to the left and looked out. He saw darkness, broken by bright hard little dots of painful light. At the bottom of the viewplate, just barely visible, hung a small green ball with the outlines of Europe and Asia still visible. It looked like a geographical globe. At some distance away hung a smaller pockmarked ball.

Everything seemed frozen and terribly silent, like a Christmas-card scene.

In a hushed voice Kennedy said, "Are we in space?"

"We sure are. You slept through the whole thing, it seems. Blast-off and null-g and everything. We're a half-day out from Earth. From here till Ganymede it's all a pretty placid downhill coast, Mr. Kennedy."

"Is it safe to get out of this cradle?" he asked.

Hills shrugged. "Why not?"

"I won't float, or anything?"

"Three hours ago we imparted spin along the longitudinal axis, Mr. Kennedy. The gravity in here is precisely one g Earth-norm. If you're hungry, food's on in the galley up front."

He ate. Ship food—packaged synthetics, nourishing and healthfully balanced and about as tasty as straw briquettes. He ate silently and alone, serving himself; the rest of the men had already had their midday meal.

Four of them were playing cards in the fore cubicle that looked out onto the stars. Kennedy was both shocked and amused when he stepped through the unlocked door and saw the four of them, grimy and bearded, dressed in filthy fatigue uniforms, squatting around an empty fuel drum playing poker with savage intensity, while five feet away from them all the splendor of the skies lay unveiled.

He had no desire to break into the game, and they ignored him so thoroughly that it was clear he was not invited. He turned away, smiling. No doubt after you made enough trips, he thought, the naked wonder of space turned dull on you, and poker remained eternally fascinating. The sight of an infinity of blazing suns was finite in its appeal, Kennedy decided. But he himself stared long and hard at the sharp blackness outside, broken by the stream of stars and by the distant redness of what he supposed was Mars.

Mars receded. Kennedy thought he caught sight of ringed Saturn later in the day. Hours passed. He ate again, slept, read.

Two days went by, or maybe three. To the six men of the crew, he was just a piece of cargo—ambulatory, perhaps, but still cargo. He read several books. He let his beard grow until the stubbly shoots began to itch fiercely, and then he shaved it off. Once he started to write a letter

67

to Marge, but he never finished it. He wished bitterly he had brought Watsinski or Dinoli or Bullard along to live on this cramped ship and see Ganymede at first hand.

Even he grew tired of the splendor of the skies. He remembered a time in his boyhood when an uncle had given him a cheap microscope, and he had gone to a nearby park and scooped up a flask of stagnant water. For days he had stared in open-mouthed awe at paramecia and fledgling snails and a host of ciliated creatures, and then the universe in the drop of water had merely given him eyestrain and, bored with his host of creatures, he had impatiently flushed them down the drain.

It was much the same here. The stars were glorious, but even sheer glory palls at length. He could meditate only so long on the magnitude of space, on the multiplicity of suns, on the strange races that might circle red Antares or bright Capella. The vastness of space held a sheerly emotional kind of wonder for him, rather than intellectual, and so it easily became exhausting and finally commonplace. He turned away from the port and returned to his books.

Until finally great Jupiter blotted out the sky, and Sizer came by to tell him that the icy crescent sliver he saw faintly against the mighty planet's bulk was their destination, Ganymede.

Again he was strapped into the cradle—the deceleration cradle, now; a mild semantic difference. A second time he took a pill, and a second time he slept. When he woke, some time later, there was whiteness outside the port—the endless eye-numbing whiteness of the snowfields of Ganymede.

It was day—"day" being a ghostly sort of half-dusk, at this distance from the sun. Kennedy knew enough about the mechanics of Ganymede from his pseudo-colony work of the past month to be aware that a Ganymedean day lasted slightly more than seven Earth days, the length of time it took Ganymede to revolve once about Jupiter—for Ganymede, like Earth's Moon, kept the same face toward its primary at all times.

Jupiter now was a gibbous splinter from dayside, a vast chip of a planet that seemed to be falling toward Ganymede's bleak surface like a celestial spear. Visible against the big planet's bulk was the lesser splinter of one of the other Galilean moons—Io, most likely, Kennedy thought.

No doubt the dome was on the other side of the ship. From his port, nothing was visible but the ugly teeth of broken mountains, bare, tufted with layers of frozen ammonia, misted by swirling methane clouds.

The ship's audio system barked. "All hands in suits! Mr. Kennedy, come forward, on the double. We've arrived on Ganymede."

Kennedy wondered how they were going to transport him without a suit. His question was answered before it could be asked; Sizer and one of the crewmen came toward him, swinging the hollow bulk of a spacesuit between them like an eviscerated corpse.

They helped him into it, clamped down the helmet, and switched on his breathing unit and his audio.

Sizer said, "You won't be in this thing long. Don't touch any of the gadgets and try not to sneeze. If you feel your breathing supply going bad, yell and yell *fast*. Everything clear?"

"Yes," Kennedy said. He felt warm and humid in the suit; they hadn't bothered to switch on his air-conditioners, or perhaps there weren't any. He saw men starting down the catwalk in their suits, and he advanced toward the yawning airlock, moving in a stiff, awkward robot-shuffle until he discovered the suit was flexible enough to allow him to walk normally.

He lowered himself through the lock and with great care descended the catwalk. He saw a sprawling low dome to his right, housing several slipshod prefabricated buildings. A truck had popped through an airlock in the side of the dome and was heading toward them. He saw a few figures inside the dome peering curiously outward at the newly arrived spaceship.

A sharp wind whistled about him; paradoxically, he was sweating inside his suit, but he also sensed the numbing cold that was just a fraction of an inch away from his skin. In the wan daylight he could see the cold outlines of stars bridging the blue-black sky. He realized that he had never actually visualized Ganymede despite all his press releases and publicity breaks.

It was a hard bitter place where the wind mumbled obscenities in his spacesuit's audio pickup and the stars glimmered in the daylight. He looked into the distance, wondering if any of the natives were on hand to witness the new arrival, but as far as he could see the landscape was barren and empty.

The truck arrived. Within its sealed pressurized cab rode a red-bearded man who signaled for them to climb into the back. They did, Kennedy going up next to last and needing a boost from the man behind him to make it. He felt helpless and ashamed of himself.

The truck turned and headed toward the opening airlock of the Ganymede dome.

10

HE FELT penned in, inside the dome. He met the sixteen men who lived there, who had lived there ever since Corporation money and Corporation skill and Corporation spaceships had let man reach Ganymede. He shifted uneasily from foot to foot, breathing the sharp, faintly acrid synthetic atmosphere of the dome, feeling mildly queasy-stomached at the lessened pull of gravity. Ganymede exerted only eighty-one percent of Earth's pull on him. He weighed just about one hundred forty-two pounds here.

He half expected to see the big figure of Colony Director Lester Brookman come striding out of the dimness to shake his hand and welcome him to Ganymede, but Brookman was just a myth he had invented one rainy May afternoon. The real head of the Ganymede outpost was a stubby little man with a bushy, gray-flecked beard. His name was Gunther. He was a third-level man in the Corporation, but up here all such titles went by the board.

He eyed Kennedy stolidly after Kennedy had disencumbered himself of his spacesuit. Finally he said, "You're Kennedy?"

"That's right."

"Papers say you'll be here until the ship returns to Earth. That's three Gannydays from now, a little over three weeks. You'll be living in Barracks B on the second level; one of the men will show you where your bunk is. There's to be no smoking anywhere in the dome at any time. If you have any questions concerning operations here, you're to ask me. If you're told by any member of this base that a given area is restricted, you're not to enter it under any circumstance. Clear?"

"Clear," Kennedy said. He resented the brusqueness of Gunther's manner, but perhaps that was what six months or a year of life on a frozen waste of a world did to a man.

"Do you know how to use a spacesuit?"

"No."

"As expected. You'll receive instruction starting at 0900 tomorrow. You'll undergo a daily drill in spacesuit technique until you've mastered its functions. We never know when the dome's going to crack."

He said it flatly and quietly, as if he might be saying, *We never know when it may start to rain.* Kennedy nodded without commenting.

"You'll be taken on a tour of the area as soon as you request it, provided there's a man free to accompany you. Under no circumstances are you to leave the dome alone. This is definite."

"When will I get a chance to meet some of the aliens?" Kennedy asked.

Gunther seemed to look away. "You'll be allowed to meet the Gannys at such time as we see fit, Mr. Kennedy. Are there any further questions?"

There were, but Kennedy didn't feel like asking them. He shook his head instead, and Gunther signaled to another member of the outpost to show him to his room.

It turned out to be a crude little box with a window opening out onto the little courtyard between the three buildings of the dome; it had a hard cot covered with a single sheet, a washstand, a baggage rack. It looked like nothing so much as a cheap hotel room in a rundown section of an old city. It was very Earthlike, and there was nothing alien about it except the view that could be had

71

by peering around the facing barracks-building at the bleak snowfields.

The three outpost buildings had been prefabricated, of course; building materials did not lie around on Ganymede waiting for visiting spacemen to shape them into neat cottages. A central ventilator system kept the dome and all the rooms within it reasonably fresh. A central power system supplied light and heat; the plumbing in the dome was crude but effective.

The entire project now attained reality for the first time for Kennedy. Despite the movies, despite research, despite everything, Ganymede had just been a name. Now it was a real place. The campaign acquired an extra dimension. This was a little planet, inhabited by intelligent beings, rich in radioactive ores, desired by a vast Corporation. He could grasp each concrete clause firmly now.

This was the place he had been selling to the world. Up here lived Lester Brookman and David Hornsfall and all his other imaginary colonists. They were myths; but Ganymede was real.

A spaceman named Jaeckel drilled him in the use of a spacesuit, showed him how to manipulate the controls that blew his nose and wiped his forehead and ventilated the suit. At the end of the first hour he had a fair idea of how to run the suit, though he was still vague on what to do when the powerpak ran dry, and how to send long-distance S O S signals through his helmet amplifier.

Once he had mastered the suit, they let him go outside the dome, always in the company of an off-duty outpost man. The snow was thick and firmly packed into ice; bare patches of rock thrust snouts up here and there. A paraffin lake was located half a mile west of the dome—a broad, dull-looking body of dark liquid. Kennedy stood at its shore and peered downward.

"Does anything live in it?"

"Snails and toads and things. The Ganymedean equivalent, of course. Methane breathers, you know. We see them come hopping up on shore during the big storms."

"How about fish equivalents?" Kennedy asked.

"We don't know. We don't have any boats and we don't have any fishing tackle. Radar says there's a few shapes moving down at the bottom but we haven't had time to find them yet."

Kennedy leaned forward, hoping to catch sight of a methane-breathing fish snouting through the depths, but all he saw was his own reflected image, shown dimly by the faint light, a bulky, grotesque, spacesuited figure with a domed head.

He was taken out to see the vegetation, too: the "forests" of scraggly waxen bushes, geared to the ammonia-methane respiratory cycle. They were inches high, with thick rigid leaves spread flat to catch as much of the sunlight as they could, and even the strongest winds failed to disturb them where they grew along a snow-banked hillside.

Inside the dome, Kennedy had little to do. After he had seen the compact turbines that powered the outpost, after he had inspected the kitchen and the game room and the little library, there was not much else for him to see. On the third day he asked Gunther when he'd be allowed to see the inhabitants of Ganymede, and Gunther had irritably responded, "Soon!"

Kennedy became suspicious. He wondered whether the Ganymedeans were not hoaxes too, along with Dr. Hornsfall and Director Brookman.

He spoke with an angular, faded-looking man named Engel, who was a linguist in Corporation employ. Engel was working on the Ganymedean language.

"It's fairly simple," he told Kennedy. "The Gannys haven't ever developed a written culture, and a language limited to oral transmission doesn't usually get to be very complex. It starts off as a series of agreed-upon grunts and it generally stays that way. The Gannys we've met have a vocabulary of perhaps a thousand active words and a residual vocabulary no bigger than three or four thousand. The language agglutinates—that is, the words pile up. There's one word for *man;* but instead of having a separate word, like *warrior,* for the concept *man-with-spear,* their word for *warrior* is simply *manwithspear.* And the grammar's ridiculously simple too—no inflections or declensions, no variation in terms of gender or case. The Gannys are lucky; they aren't saddled with the confused remnants of the old Indo-Aryan protolanguage the way we are. It's a terribly simple language."

"Meaning that they're terribly simple people?" Kennedy asked.

Engel laughed. "It's not quite a one-to-one correlation. Matter of fact, they're damned quick thinkers, and they get along pretty well despite the handicap of such a limited language. It's a limited world. You don't need many words on a planet where there's hardly any seasonal change and where living conditions remain uniform century after century. Uniformly miserable, I mean."

Kennedy nodded. Engel showed him a mimeographed pamphlet he had prepared, labelled *Notes Toward A Ganny Etymology and Philology*.

"Mind if I look this over?" Kennedy asked.

Engel shrugged and said, "I guess it's all right. It can't do any harm to let you read it."

Kennedy studied the pamphlet alone in his room that night, for lack of any better recreation. He fell asleep with the light on and the book still open, after a couple of hours of mumbling disjointed Ganny phrases which he hoped followed Engel's phonetic system; he didn't even notice it when the room-light cut off, as it did every night at 0100 camp-time.

On the fourth day a tremendous storm swept in and engulfed the area. Kennedy stood in the yard near the arching curve of the dome, staring out in awe at the fierce torrent of precipitated ammonia that poured down on the plain, giving way finally to feathery clouds of ammonia-crystal snow and then, at last, to silence. The plain was covered with a fresh fall, now, and after it came the irascible wind, sculpturing the new fall into fantastic spires and eddies. Snow dunes heaped high against the side of the dome, and a trio of men in spacesuits went outside to clear them away. In the distance he saw the spaceship still upright, its landing vanes concealed by fresh snow, its dark prow tipped with mounds of white.

And on the fifth day he was again alone in his room when a tattoo of knocks sounded. He slipped Engel's linguistics pamphlet under his soggy pillow and opened the door.

Spaceman Jaeckel stood there. "Gunther sent me to get you, Kennedy. Some aliens are here. They're waiting outside the dome if you want to meet them."

Hastily he ran downstairs, found the spacesuit rack, and

donned his. Gunther was already in his, looking small and round and agile.

"On the double, if you want to see them, Kennedy! They aren't going to wait out there forever!"

Four of them went through the lock—Gunther, Engel, Kennedy, and a spaceman named Palmer. Kennedy felt a strange tingle of excitement. These were the beings the Steward and Dinoli agency was training mankind to hate; these were the beings Alf Haugen was gradually building up as enemies of humanity, and he was going to meet them now.

There were three of them, standing in a little group ten feet from the airlock entrance. Naked except for their cloth girdles, noseless, eyes hooded, they looked to Kennedy like aborigines of some bizarre South Sea Island as seen in a dream. Their skin, pale white, had a waxy sheen to it. Their mouths were glum, sagging semicircles, lipless. At first Kennedy was surprised that they could bear the murderous cold, standing in calm nudity with no sign of discomfort.

But why the hell shouldn't they, he thought. *This is their world. They breathe its foul, corrosive air and they brush their teeth, if they have teeth, with the high-octane stuff that flows in their lakes and rivers. They probably can't understand how we can possibly survive in the blazing heat of Earth, and drink that poisonous hydrogen-oxygen compound we're so fond of.*

"These three are from the closest tribe," Gunther said. "They live eleven miles to the east and come here every seventh Earth-day to talk to us."

And indeed they *were* talking; one of them began speaking in a low monotone, addressing his words to Gunther. Fascinated, Kennedy listened.

He could only pick out a word here and there; his few hours spent with Engel's booklet had not made him a master of the language. But the words he picked out interested him greatly.

For the alien seemed to be saying, ". . . once again . . . leave us . . . hatecarryingbeings . . . interfere . . . when you go . . . soon . . . ."

Gunther replied with a rapid-fire string of syllables spoken with such machine-gun intensity that Kennedy could scarcely catch the meaning of a single word. He did pick

75

up one, though; it was the Ganny word for total negation, absolute refusal.

The alien replied, ". . . sadness . . . pain . . . until go . . . sacrilege . . ."

"Mind if I ask what the conversation's all about?" Kennedy said.

Engel blinked. Gunther tightened his lips, then said, "We're arranging for transportation of supplies to the alien village in exchange for a bit of negotiation for mining rights with the village chief. He's telling us the best time of day to make the delivery."

Kennedy tried to hide his surprise. Either Gunther had just reeled off a flat lie, or else Kennedy had been completely wrong in his translation of the conversation. It had seemed to him that the aliens had been demanding an Earth evacuation, and that Gunther had been refusing. But perhaps he had been wrong; not even the simplest of languages could be learned in a matter of days.

The aliens were stirring restlessly. The spokesman repeated his original statement twice, then tipped his head back in a kind of ceremonial gesture, leaned forward, and exhaled a white cloud. Ammonia crystals formed briefly on the face-plate of Gunther's breathing-helmet. The Corporation man replied with a sentence too terse for Kennedy to be able to translate.

Then the aliens nodded their heads and uttered the short disyllable that meant farewell; Kennedy caught it clearly. Automatically the response-word floated up from his memory, and he said it: "Ah-*yah.*" The other three Earthmen spoke the word at the same time. The aliens turned and gravely stalked away into the whirling wind.

A moment later Gunther whirled and seized Kennedy's arm tightly with his spacegloved hand. Through the breathing mask Gunther's face assumed an almost demonic intensity as he glared at Kennedy.

"What did you say?" he demanded. "What did you just say? Did I just hear you say a word to that Ganny in his own language? *Where did you learn it? Who authorized you to learn Ganny?* I could have you shot for this, Kennedy—agency pull or no agency pull!"

11

For a moment Kennedy stood frozen, listening to the fierce wind swirl around him, not knowing what to say. By revealing his knowledge of Ganymedean he had committed a major blunder.

"Well?" Gunther demanded. "How come you speak Ganny?"

"I—"

He stopped. Engel came to his rescue.

"That's the only word he knows," the tall linguist said. "Couple of days ago he was visiting me and when he left I said good-bye to him in Ganny. He wanted to know what I had just said, and I told him. There's no harm in that, Gunther."

Uncertainly the outpost chief released his grip on Kennedy's arm. Kennedy realized Engel was saving his own skin as well as his by the lie; evidently it was out of bounds for him to speak the native tongue.

But he saw his advantage. "Look here, Gunther—I'm not a Corporation man and I'm only technically under your command. Where do you come off threatening to shoot me for saying good-bye to a Ganny in his own language? I could let Bullard know and he'd bounce you down to tenth-level for a stunt like that."

In a short sharp sentence Gunther expressed his opinion of Corporation Executive Bullard. Then he said, "Let's go back into the dome. This is no place to stand around having a chat."

Without waiting for further discussion he signaled to have the lock opened. Kennedy was more than happy to turn his back on the bleakness of the open Ganymedean field.

They stripped off their spacesuits in silence, and racked them. Gunther said, "Suppose we go to my quarters, Kennedy. We can talk about things there."

"Should I come too?" Engel asked.

"No, you get about your business. And watch out how much classified info you teach to visitors next time, Mr. Engel. Clear?"

"Clear," Engel muttered, and turned away.

Gunther's quarters proved to be considerably more auspicious than the other rooms under the dome. A wide window gave unrestricted view of the entire area, but could be opaqued at the touch of a button; the cot was general issue and ascetic, but extra ventilator controls and brighter room lights indicated to Kennedy that Gunther was no subscriber to the theory that a commanding officer should share every privation of his men.

He opened a closet and took out a half-empty bottle of liquor. The label had been removed and a new one substituted, reading *Property of Robert Gunther.*

"Care for a drink?"

Kennedy did not, but he nodded deliberately. "Sure. Don't mind if I do. Straight?"

"There's ice," Gunther said. He fixed the drink, handed it to Kennedy, and said, "I'm sorry I blew up over such a little thing out there. You have to understand what life's like here, Kennedy. It's not easy on the nerves. Not at all. I try to maintain discipline over myself as well as the others, but there are times when my nerves just pop. I'm sorry it had to happen to you, that's all."

Kennedy smiled. "You practically ordered me off to the firing squad because I knew a word of Ganny. How come the language's so top-secret?"

It was a telling question. Gunther shifted uneasily and said, "It isn't, really. It's merely that we want to make sure all Earth-Ganymede negotiations take place through the Corporation. We wouldn't want another outfit to set up shop here and try to cut in."

"Meaning, presumably, that you suspect I'm going to learn the language, compile a dictionary of Ganny when I get back to Earth, and sell it for a fabulous sum to some as-yet-nonexistent competitor of the Extraterrestrial Development and Exploration Corporation, Ganymede Division? I assure you I've got no such sinister intentions. I'm just a hapless public relations man sent up here by his boss to get the feel of the territory."

"I haven't accused you of anything, Kennedy. But we have to take certain security precautions."

"I understand that."

"Good. In case you're filing a report, I'd greatly appreciate it if you'd omit any mention of this incident. As a favor to me."

"I guess I can manage that little thing," Kennedy said lightly.

He left Gunther soon after, feeling greatly perplexed. The outpost chief's real motivation seemed utterly transparent. Gunther was not fearing the advent of a rival corporation; it took years of legal work and billions in capital to build an organization the size of ED & E. No wildcat operation was going to send a ship to Ganymede to whisk mining rights out from under Gunther's sharp nose, making use of a Ganny dictionary prepared for them by Kennedy.

No, there could be only one possible reason why Gunther had reacted so violently when Kennedy had displayed a seeming understanding of Ganny. Gunther was afraid that Kennedy would overhear something the Corporation was trying to keep secret.

And that something, Kennedy suspected, was the fact that the Ganymedeans were hostile to the idea of having Earthmen settle on their world, and far from being willing to negotiate for mining rights were anxiously demanding that Gunther and his men get off.

That had seemed to be the drift of the conversation Kennedy had witnessed. And if that was the case, he thought, then the only way the Corporation was going to get what it wanted on Ganymede would be by a virtual extermination of the Gannys. No mere United Nations "police action," as Kennedy and the other agency men had been led to believe, but a full-scale bitter war of oppression.

Sure, they would rationalize it. The Gannys were a non-technological people who owned a vast horde of valuable radioactive ores and had no intentions of using them; for the public good of the solar system, then, these ores should be taken from them.

A cold thought struck him: any rationalization would

come through the agency. Once it became apparent that the Gannys would have to be forcibly hurled to the side, his job would be to sell the people of Earth on the proposition that this was a necessary and cosmically wise action.

It was a nasty business, and he had been drawn into it deeper than he suspected. Oh, he had never thought it was a lily-white enterprise, but despite Marge's quiet opposition and Spalding's bitter outbursts he had gone along with the agency unthinkingly. The agency mask had been his defense: the unthinking reservation of judgement that allowed him to enter into a contract with little concern for the questions of values tangential to it.

Well, now he was seeing it clearly and first-hand. He returned to his room, planning to study the Ganny dictionary more intently. Next week when the aliens returned he *had* to know more of the true position of things.

But his door was ajar when he reached his room, and the light was on. There were no locks on the doors, but he had hardly expected someone to just walk in. He pushed open the door.

Engel was sitting on the edge of his bed waiting for him.

Kennedy waved cheerily to him. "I guess I owe you thanks. That could have been a nasty business with Gunther out there if you hadn't said what you did."

"Yes. Look here, Kennedy—I have to have that booklet back. Immediately. Where is it?"

"Back? Why?"

"Gunther would have me flayed if he knew I gave it to you. It was really unpardonable on my part—but you seemed so interested, and I was so anxious to have you see my work and be impressed by it." The linguist flushed and looked at his shoes. "Where is it now?"

Kennedy circled behind Engel and drew the dog-eared pamphlet out from under the pillow. Engel reached for it, but Kennedy snatched it quickly away.

"Give that to me! Kennedy, don't you undersand that Gunther absolutely would execute me if he knew you had that? It's classified!"

"Why?"

"That doesn't matter. Give it to me."

Kennedy tucked it under his arm. "I don't intend to. I

80

want to study it some more. It's a very ingenious work, Engel. I *am* impressed."

"If you don't give that to me," Engel said slowly, "I'll tell Gunther that you entered my quarters when I wasn't there and *stole* it from me. I know how many copies there are supposed to be. But I don't want to have to do that, so hand it over, will you?" The linguist nibbled at his lip and flicked a globule of sweat from his forehead.

The room was very quiet a moment. Kennedy tightened his grip on the booklet under his arm. Staring levelly at Engel, he said, "You don't want to do that. I'll make a deal with you: you let me keep the dictionary, and I'll make sure Gunther never has occasion to find out you gave it to me. And I'll return it when I leave Ganymede. Otherwise, you try to tell Gunther I stole the dictionary and I'll tell him you gave it to me of your own free will, and then lied to him outside the dome just now to keep your own nose clean. It'll be my word against yours, but you'll be in a tough way trying to explain just why you took my part out there."

Engel knotted his hands nervously together. "It won't work. Gunther trusts me—"

"Like hell he does. Gunther doesn't even trust himself. Let me keep the dictionary or I'll go to Gunther right now and tell him the whole story."

Scowling, Engel said, "Okay. The dictionary's yours— but keep your mouth shut the next time you're around any Gannys. If you stop to ask a local chief the time of day, Gunther'll roast us both."

"I'll keep quiet next time," Kennedy promised.

But as it developed, "next time" did not look like too probable an event.

Three days slipped by, in Kennedy's second week on Ganymede. He spent much of his time studying Engel's little handbook of the Ganny language, and repeated phrases and sentences to himself each night in a muttered whisper that once had his next-door neighbor banging on the partition and telling him to shut up and go to sleep.

He went on jeep trips over the Ganymedean terrain; it was nighttime on Ganymede now, and would be for four more Earth-days; Jupiter hung broodingly massive in the sky, blotting out the stars. Kennedy noticed that he instinctively avoided looking up at the great swollen planet in the sky; it was too sickeningly big, too awesome, for easy viewing.

Moons danced in the sky, swimming in and out of sight with dizzy unpredictability; now Io, now Europa, now far-off Callisto came whirling by, and their orbits were a computer's nightmare. Kennedy was impressed.

The terrain was monotonous, though—endless bluish ice-fields unbroken by sign of life. Once Kennedy asked his companion if they could visit a Ganny village for a change, instead of merely rolling on over icy wastes.

"You'll have to ask Gunther about that. I don't have authority to take you there."

Kennedy asked Gunther. Gunther scowled and said, "I'm afraid not. The Ganny villages are restricted areas for visitors to the outpost."

"Why?"

"You don't ask why around here, Kennedy. You've been very cooperative up to now. Don't spoil it."

With a brusque gesture Gunther dismissed him. Kennedy turned away, his mind full of unanswered questions.

He studied his handbook. He waited impatiently for the Gannys to pay their next visit to the outpost; he wanted to listen to the conversation again, to find out exactly what the relationship was between Earthman and alien on this little world.

He asked questions of the other men—carefully guarded questions. He asked a mining engineer to take him to the main radioactives deposits. "I understand the Corporation expects to find transuranic elements in their natural state here on Ganymede," he said.

The mining engineer scratched his heavy-bearded chin and laughed. "Where'd you hear a crazy thing like that? Transuranics on Ganny? Maybe on Jupiter, but not here unless everything we know about planetary cores is cockeyed."

"But the data sheets we got implied it," Kennedy persisted. "Part of the general abundance of radioactive ores on Ganymede may be due to the presence of natural transuranics."

"You better check those data sheets again, Mister. There isn't any general abundance of hot stuff on Ganny. You can track that snow for days with your gamma detector and not get a peep."

That was interesting, Kennedy thought. Because if Ganymede was not as rich in radioactives as the Corporation publicity puffs had intimated, and if the natives were bluntly opposed to Terran operations on Ganymede, then the whole agency-nurtured maneuver was nothing more or less than a naked power grab on the part of the Corporation, a set-up maneuver that would drag the U.N. in to conquer Ganymede at no expense to the Corporation and then hand the little world over to Bullard and Company on a chrome-plated platter.

But he had to have more proof. He had to speak to the natives first-hand, preferably without any of Gunther's men around.

The day before the expected visit of the Gannys, Kennedy happened to mention to Gunther that he was looking forward to seeing the aliens again.

"Oh? You haven't heard? The visit's been called off. It's some sort of holy season in the village and they've decided not to see any Earthmen till it's over."

"And when will that be?"

"Five Ganny days from now. A little more than a month, Earth-time."

That was interesting too, Kennedy thought. Because that meant he would have no further opportunity at all for seeing or listening to the Gannys. And this "some sort of holy season" sounded too slick, too patently contrived, to be convincing.

No. Gunther simply did not want him to penetrate Corporation activities on Ganymede any deeper than he already had. Evidently Dinoli and Bullard had misjudged Kennedy, thinking he was much less observant than he actually was, or they would never have let him go to Ganymede and possibly discover all manner of uncomfortable things.

There was only a week left to his stay now. He knew he would have to move quickly and efficiently in his remaining time, if he were to discover the underlying facts of the Ganymede operation.

He disliked blackmail. But in this case there was no help for it. He went to see Engel.

12

THE LINGUIST was not happy to see him. He greeted him unsmilingly and said, "What do you want, Kennedy?"

With elaborate care Kennedy shut the door and took a seat facing Engel. "The first thing I want is absolute silence on your part. If a word of what I tell you now gets back to Gunther or anyone else, I'll kill you."

Just like that. And at the moment, Kennedy believed he would, too.

Engel said, "Go ahead. Talk."

"I want you to do me a favor. I want you to get me one of those jeeps and fix things so I can go out alone during sleep-time tonight."

"Kennedy, this is preposterous. I—"

"You nothing. Either I get the jeep or I tell Gunther you're a subversive who deliberately gave me the Ganny dictionary and who tipped me off on a few of the lesser-known gambits the Corporation's engaging in. I can lie damn persuasively, Engel; it's my business."

Engel said nothing. Kennedy noticed that the man's fingernails had been bitten ragged. He felt sorry for the unfortunate linguist, but this was no time for pity; the Corporation showed none, and neither could he.

"Do I get the jeep?"

Engel remained silent.

Finally he pulled in his breath in a sobbing sigh and said, "Yes, damn you."

"Without any strings?"

Engel nodded.

Kennedy rose. "Thanks, Engel. And listen: I don't want you to get hurt in this business. I'm doing what I'm doing because I need to do it, and I'm stepping on your neck because it's the only neck I can step on—but I'm sorry about the whole filthy business. If everything goes well, Gunther'll never find out about the dictionary or the jeep."

"Save the apologies," Engel said. "When do you want the jeep?"

Kennedy left after dark-out time that night; the dome was shrouded in night, and the faint illumination afforded by Io and the larger radiation that was Jupiter's light only served to cast conflicting and obscuring shadows over the outpost. He locked himself into the jeep's pressurized cab, made sure his spacesuit was in order, checked the ammunition supply for the gun he had borrowed, made sure he had remembered the dictionary. Engel led him through the lock.

"Remember now," he radioed back. "I'm going to be back here at 0600. Be damn sure you're here to let me in, and that you're alone."

"I'll be here," Engel said. "Alone, I hope."

The Ganny village was eleven miles to the east of the outpost. Kennedy knew that the aliens had a thirty-two hour sleep-wake cycle, and he hoped that his visit would find them awake; otherwise he might not have another opportunity to speak to them.

He had no difficulty operating the jeep; it was equipped with compass and distance guide, and no more than twenty minutes after he had left the Terran outpost he saw what could only be the alien village, nestling between two cruel rock fangs. It was located, logically enough, along one shore of a broad river of fast-flowing hydrocarbons. The houses were clusters of small, dome-shaped igloos put together out of bluish ice-blocks, and there were aliens moving to and fro in the settlement as he drew near. He saw them stop their work and peer suspiciously into the darkness at him.

He cut the jeep's engines a hundred yards from the edge of the river, activated his spacesuit, strapped on his gun, pocketed the dictionary, and stepped outside. He walked toward the river, where half a dozen aliens were casting nets or dangling lines.

As he approached he saw one man yank forth his line with a catch—a thick-bodied fish-like creature with fierce red eyes and short fleshy fins. There was no look of triumph on the man's face as he waded ashore and deposited his catch on a heap of similar fish caught earlier. This was food, not sport, and there was no occasion for triumph if a catch was made—only sadness if one were not.

The aliens looked alike to Kennedy. He wondered if there were some way of finding the three who had visited the outpost the week before.

"I am a friend," he said slowly and clearly, in the Ganny tongue.

They gathered hesitantly about him, those who were not too busy with their nets and their lines. He looked from one noseless, grotesque face to the next, and hoped they were better at telling one Earthman from another than he was at discerning alien identities.

They were. One said, "You are a new one."

"I am. I come to talk with you."

"It is the food-gathering time. We must work. One will come from the village to talk with you."

Kennedy looked sharply at the ring of aliens. They were stocky beings, not quite his height, lumpy-bodied, with thick, six-fingered hands and practically no necks. They were not human. It was strange to stand here in below-zero temperature on a world whose air was poison to his lungs, and talk with unhuman creatures. Nightmarish.

Another alien was coming from the village toward him. At first glance he seemed indistinguishable from all the others, but then Kennedy saw that this one had an air of authority about him that set him apart.

"You must not disturb the fishermen," the new one said as he drew near. "Their job is sacred. Who are you?"

"I come from back there."

"I know that. But you are not like the others."

"I am not a friend of the other men who come to you," Kennedy said.

"Then they will kill you. They kill those who are not their friends."

"Have they killed any of your people?"

"No. But they say they will if we do not give them welcome here. We ask them to leave. To go back to the sky. But they say they will bring others of their kind here soon. We will not oppose this, but it grieves us."

They walked away from the busy fishermen. Kennedy struggled to catch the alien's words, and realized the Ganny was speaking with special care. The spokesman said, "Your people do not understand us. This is our land. Our tribe chose this as its dying-ground hundreds of hundred-days ago. We ask them to go, or to move to another clan-ground. But they will not go. They say they will stay, and will bring many hands of hands more of their numbers from the sky. And they will not let us teach them."

"Teach them?" Kennedy repeated. "Teach them what?"

"The way of life. Respect for existence. Understanding of the currents of beingness." The complex phrases made Kennedy frown, bewildered. "They think we are simple fishermen," said the alien. "This is correct. But we are more than fishermen. We have a civilization. We have no guns and no space-vessels; we did not need them. But we have other things."

Kennedy found himself becoming deeply interested. He squatted down on a barrel-shaped projection of ice and said, "Tell me about these things."

"We have no books, none of the fine things you Earthmen have. Our world does not allow such luxuries. But we have developed other things, compensations. A language —you find it easy to understand?"

Kennedy nodded.

"Our language is the work of many minds over many years. Its simplicity caused us much pain to achieve. Do you have much time to spend with us?"

He looked at the chronometer in the wrist of his spacesuit. The time was only 0230; he had three hours yet before it was time to return to the outpost. He told the alien that.

"Good. Our next sleep-time is when the silvery moon has set. Until the time for you to leave, we can talk. I think you will listen."

The silvery moon meant high-albedo Europa. Kennedy tried to remember the schedule. Europa would set toward "morning," some six or seven hours from now.

The alien spoke, and for the next three hours Kennedy listened in wonder. When the alien was through, Kennedy realized why Gunther had not been anxious for him to see the Gannys too closely.

They were far from being mere primitive savages. They had a culture perhaps older than Earth's. The bleak barrenness of their world had made it impossible for them to develop a technology, but in compensation they had created an incredible oral tradition of poetry and philosophy.

Kennedy received a brief sketch. The philosophy was one of resignation, of calm understanding of the inexorable absolute laws of the universe. It was inevitable that a people living under conditions such as these would develop a philosophy that counseled them to accept in gratitude whatever came to them.

They were people who knew how to wait, and how to accept defeat. People who knew how to hope, even when menacing invaders from beyond the sky came to threaten.

They had a poetry, too; Kennedy listened, and wondered. Their language was awesomely simple, with a simplicity born of centuries of polishing, and the poetry was evocative and many-leveled, so far as Kennedy could penetrate it at first hearing. Everything was oral. He had never believed that a race without a written culture could achieve such things, but he had never known a race living on such a world.

He was reluctant to leave, when the time came. But he knew there would be grave consequences otherwise, so he made his apologies, breaking the spell cast by the alien being, and headed for his jeep.

At about 0530 he began driving back westward toward the outpost. In the quiet alien night the snowfields sparkled and glittered with the reflected light of half a dozen moons; it was a lovely sight, and, inside the warm pressurized cab of the jeep, he felt none of the brutality of the conditions outside, only the silent beauty.

But there was nothing beautiful about the Corporation scheme, he thought. He wondered if he could ever purge himself of the taint of the last two months' work.

He thought of Marge's gradual withdrawal from him as he became more and more involved in the Ganymede contract, and of Spalding's cynical condemnation of the project at the same time as his continued work on it. Well, Spalding had his reasons. And at least he had seen through the plan, instead of blithely accepting it the way Kennedy had done.

The Corporation was using the U.N. as its cat's-paw. Ganymede was likely territory for exploitation—the Earth had no more simple races left, no more technologically backward areas, thanks to a century of intensive development, but there still were other worlds for fast-working promoters to conquer.

Ganymede, for instance.

The Gannys had a rich and wonderful culture—anyone could see that given an hour's contact with them. So the Corporation would have to suppress that fact, or else there would be interference with its plans. Thanks to the agency and to Kennedy's own scheme, the Gannys would be mowed down, unprotesting—for that was the essence of their philosophy—to make room for the Terran exploiters.

Unless some action were taken now.

Kennedy felt clear-headed and tranquil about the part he was going to play in the coming weeks. He would return to Earth and somehow let the world know the profound nature of the Ganymedean culture; he would prevent the slaughter before it began, as partial atonement for all he had done to foment it. Marge would understand, and would forgive him for his earlier part.

He felt bitter about the deception that had been practiced on him and which he, in turn, had helped foist on all of Earth. He had no moralizing objections to Corporation activity—but he felt strongly that a culture such as he had just been shown should be preserved, and learned from. The Gannys had much to teach to an Earth caught in endless internal turmoil. He intended to visit them every night until the time came to return to Earth.

And when he was back on Earth he could reveal the truth. It isn't everyone, he thought, who has the chance to repair damage he's helped create. But I have a glittering opportunity.

The Gannys would never fight back. Armed resistance was not part of their way. But if he could prevent the conflict from ever beginning . . .

He would have to move carefully, though. He was taking on a mighty antagonist in the Corporation.

Engel was waiting inside the airlock as Kennedy brought the jeep up, at 0559 hours. Right on time. The linguist looked pale and tense; Kennedy wondered if there were some trap waiting for him. Gunther, maybe, with armed men.

He drew his gun. The airlock slid open and he guided the jeep through. Springing from the jeep, he made sure he had his gun out and ready.

"You can put the blunderbuss away," Engel whispered. "Everything's clear."

Kennedy looked around. "No one knows I've been gone? No one missed me?"

"They've all been sleeping like babes," Engel said. "All except me. I've been sitting in my room staring at the walls all night. Where the devil did you go, Kennedy? And why?"

"That's hardly public concern, as they say. Help me off with my suit."

Engel assisted him as he climbed out of the bulky protective suit. Kennedy turned to the linguist and stared quietly at him for a long moment.

"I went to visit the Gannys tonight," he said. "I spent three hours listening to a disquisition on Ganny philosophy and hearing some Ganny poetry. These people aren't as primitive as Gunther seems to think they are, Engel."

"I don't know what you're talking about."

"You're lying. You've spoken to the Gannys. You know that their language is a marvel of communication. You know about their philosophy and their poetry and their outlook on life. And you intend to sit back and let all these things be blotted from the universe forever."

Engel's jaw tightened. He said nothing.

"Well," Kennedy went on, "*I* don't. And I'm going to do something about it, or at least try to do something, when I get back to Earth. And while I'm here I'm going to soak up as much Ganny thinking as I possibly can. It's good for the soul, Engel. You'll help me."

"I don't want to be a party to your crazy schemes, Kennedy."

"I want you to help me. For once in your life you can do something worthwhile. More worthwhile than making lists of intransitive verbs, anyway."

13

Two DAYS that were not days, two nights that were not nights, while the greater darkness of the Ganymedean night cloaked the outpost for the full twenty-four hours of the arbitrarily designated "day." And in that time Kennedy saw the Ganny chieftain twice.

He told Engel, "You arrange with Gunther that you get assigned to take me out on my daily tour of the snow dunes and local lakes. Only we'll go to the village instead of rubbernecking around the hills."

Engel was unwilling. Engel scowled and grimaced and tried to think of reasons why the idea was dangerous, but in the end he gave in, because he was a weak man and both he and Kennedy knew it. Kennedy had long since mastered the art of manipulating people *en masse;* now he was manipulating one single man, and succeeding at it.

He had five days left on Ganymede. He knew he had to make the most of them.

During the following day Engel came to him and told him to get ready for his daily drive. They skirted the hills and the big lake west of the camp, then swerved one hundred eighty degrees and tracked straight for the Ganny village.

They spent two hours there. The old leader explained the Ninefold Way of Righteousness to them, the essence of the Ganny moral code. Kennedy listened and memorized as much as he could—letting it soak in, because he knew it was good and workable—and occasionally glanced at Engel, and saw that the linguist was not blind to the wonders of these people.

"You see what kind of people they are?" Kennedy demanded, as they rode back to the outpost.

"Sure I see what they are," Engel grunted. "I've known it from the start."

"And yet you'll stand by while they're being wiped out by Terran forces who've been deluded into thinking they're killing hostile alien demons?"

"What can I do about it?" Engel asked sullenly. "I'm a Corporation linguist. I don't argue with what the Corporation wants to do. I just think about it, inside, and keep my mouth shut."

Of course you do, Kennedy thought. *The way we all do. But for once I can't sit by and collect my check and let this thing happen. I have to stand up and fight.*

He wondered what Gunther would say when he found out that the visiting public relations man was engaged in a highly subversive series of contacts with the Gannys. The little man would have an apoplectic fit, certainly.

Kennedy found out soon enough. He had been making notes of what he recalled of the old man's talks, scribbling down his recollections of Ganny poetry and fragments of the philosophical discussions. He kept these notes hidden in his room. But on the fourth day, when he went for them to add some notes on Ganny ideas of First Cause, he found they were missing.

For a moment he felt thundering alarm. Then he thought, in a deliberate attempt to calm himself, *Engel must have borrowed them. Sure. Engel borrowed them.*

There was a knock on the door. Kennedy opened it.

Gunther stood there. Gripped tightly in his hand was Kennedy's little sheaf of notes. His eyes were bleak and cold.

"Would you mind telling me what the hell these things are?" he demanded.

Kennedy struggled for self-control. "Those? Those are my notes. For my work, I mean. Research and comments to help me in my project."

Gunther did not smile. "I've read them. They are notes on Ganny culture, philosophy, and poetry. You've been seeing the Gannys secretly."

"And what if I have?"

"You've been violating a direct order of mine. This is a military-discipline base. We don't allow orders to be violated."

"Give me my notes," Kennedy said.

"I'm keeping them. They'll be sent back to Earth to the Corporation heads, as evidence against you. You're under arrest."

"On what charge?"

"Espionage against the Corporation," Gunther said flatly.

Two spacemen of the outpost locked him away in a brig down below, and left him in a windowless little room. He stared glumly at the metal walls. Somehow, he had expected this. He had been risking too much by visiting the Gannys. But listening to them had been like taking drugs; for the first time he had found a philosophy that gave him hope in a world that seemed to be without hope. He had wanted desperately to spend every one of his few remaining days on Ganymede in the village.

The day passed. Night came, and he was fed and the door was locked again. Gunther was taking no chances. They would pen him up in here until the time came to ship him back to Earth.

He tried to sleep. For the past few days he had been getting along on two and three hours of sleep each twenty-four hour period, stealing out each night to visit the Gannys, and he was showing it; his feet felt leaden, his eyes stung. He had been subsisting on no-sleep tabs and catching naps at odd moments when he felt he could get away with it. But now he could not sleep.

His watch said 0330 when he heard the bolt outside his door being opened. He looked up. Maybe it was Gunther coming to extract some kind of "confession."

Engel entered.

"I got put on guard duty," the linguist said. "Gunther wants you watched round the clock."

Kennedy looked at him bleakly. "Why did you come in here? To keep me company?"

"I wanted to tell you that I had nothing to do with his finding out. He's just a suspicious man. He had your room searched while you were out, and he found your notes. I'm sorry."

I'm sorry too, Kennedy thought. *Because now I'll go back to Earth under guard, and I won't ever get my chance to expose things.*

He said, "Did you ever go back to the village to explain why we didn't show up for your next session?"

"No. I was afraid to."

An idea formed in Kennedy's mind. "How about letting me out now? We can borrow a jetsled. Everyone's asleep. At least we can warn the Gannys of what's happened. You can bring me back here and lock me up again in the morning."

"It's too risky. Gunther suspects me as it is," Engel said.

But Kennedy knew his man. It took him only a few minutes more of persuasion to break down Engel's resistance. Together they donned spacesuits and headed out to the area where the outpost's jetsleds were kept. Kennedy was bursting with impatience to see the villagers once again. He realized he had violated a prime rule of the Ganny way by compelling Engel to release him, but this was no time for passive resistance. There was time to put the Ganny philosophy into operation later, when the survival of the Gannys was assured.

"Set the airlock to automatic open-close and let's get out of here," Kennedy called to Engel. "We don't have all night."

The face behind Engel's breathing-helmet was stiff and tense. Engel had never entered into any of this with full willingness, Kennedy thought; it was always partly because he thought Kennedy was right, partly because he was being blackmailed into accompanying him.

The airlock started to slide open. Kennedy made room for Engel on the sled and rested his hand lightly on the firing switch.

Floodlights suddenly burst out blindingly all over the airlock area.

Gunther stood there, looking hard and bitter in the bright light. Behind him were three other men—Jaeckel, Palmer, Latimer.

"It had to be you, Engel," Gunther said slowly. "I figured you were the one that was helping him. That's why I put you on guard duty tonight. And I guess I was right. What the hell do you think you're up to on that sled, you two?"

Engel started to say something, something shapeless that was half a moan. Kennedy nudged him viciously with his free elbow.

"Hold on tight!" he whispered. "I'm going to get the sled started!"

"No, you can't!"

"Want to join me in the brig, then?"

"Okay," Gunther called. "Get off that sled. This time I'll make sure neither of you can get loose until that ship leaves for Earth."

"You make sure of that," Kennedy said. Calmly he threw the firing switch to full and shoved the thrust-control wide open.

The jetsled bucked and crashed forward in a sudden plunging motion, tossing a spume of yellow flame behind it. Kennedy heard Gunther's angry yell as the sled passed through the open airlock perhaps fifteen seconds before the time-control was due to close it again.

There was the quick harsh chatter of gunfire coming from behind them. Kennedy did not look back. He crouched down as low as he could on the sled, praying that none of the shots would touch off the fuel tanks behind him, and guided the little flat sled into the Ganymedean darkness.

His course was already figured. He would circle wide to the west, far out enough to mislead any pursuers, he hoped, and then head for the Ganymedean village. But after that, he had no plans.

He had bungled. And perhaps he had cost the Ganymedeans their one chance of salvation, as well as cutting his own throat, by letting Gunther find out what he was doing. He tried to regard the situation fatalistically, as a Ganny might, but could not. It was tragic, no matter how he looked at it, and it could have been avoided had he been more careful.

He forced himself not to think of what would happen to him four days hence, when the supply ship blasted off on its return trip to Earth. No doubt he and Engel would be aboard as prisoners. He had cut loose all bonds with Earth in one sudden frightful moment, and he tried not to think about it.

"I was wondering how long it would take for Gunther to get wise to what we were doing," he said after they had gone more than five miles with no sign of pursuit. "It was bound to happen eventually. But we had to do what we did, Engel. *Someone* had to do it. And it just happened that I came along and dragged you into it."

Engel did not reply. Kennedy wondered about the bitter

thoughts the linguist must be thinking. He himself had reexerted the old agency mask; he was not thinking at all, not bothering to consider the inevitably drastic consequences of his wild rebellion on Ganymede.

They fled on into the night. When he thought it was safe he changed the sled's course and headed straight for the village. He was becoming an expert at traveling over the icebound plain.

"None of it would have started if you had kept your dictionary hidden away," Kennedy said. "But you showed it to me, and I borrowed it, and I learned a couple of words of Ganny, and on a slim thread like that you're washed up with the Corporation and I'm finished with the agency. But you know something, Engel? I'm not sorry at all. Not even if they catch us and take us back to Earth and publicly disembowel us. At least we stood on our hind legs and did something we thought was *right*." He stopped to consider something. "You *did* think it was right, didn't you? I mean, you didn't help me in this thing just because I was twisting your arm? I hope you did it out of ethical reasons. It's lousy enough to throw away your career in a single week, without having done it just because some other guy with ethics came along and made you do it."

Engel still was silent. His silence began to irritate Kennedy.

"What's the matter?" he demanded. "Scared speechless? Did the fact that Gunther caught us throw you into such a blue funk you can't talk?"

Still no answer. A cold worm of panic raced around the interior of Kennedy's stomach, and he swiveled his neck to see if—

He was right.

One of Gunther's final desperate shots had ripped a neat hole in Engel's breathing-helmet. The bullet had entered on a sharp angle, puncturing the helmet just in front of the linguist's nose, grazing his left cheekbone harmlessly —it left only a thin scratch—and passing out of the helmet below Engel's left earlobe. That had been enough.

Engel's air supply must have rushed out in one moist, foaming burst. Blood had dribbled from his mouth and ears as the internal suit-pressure dropped from the 14.7 psi of the suit to the much lower external pressure. Engel's face was blotchy, puffed, swollen, eyes bulging, thin lips drawn back in a contorted, grotesque smile.

He had died in a hurry. So fast that he had not even had time to grunt an anguished last cry into his open suit-microphone. And for half an hour Kennedy had ferried a corpse across the Ganymedean wastes, talked to him and chided him, and finally had lost his patience and his temper at the corpse's continued obstinate silence.

Kennedy compressed his lips into a thin, bitter scowl. Engel had been so proud of his dictionary, so anxious to show it off to the visitor from Earth. And a couple of weeks later that dictionary had worked his death, as surely as if it had been the bullet that sent his air-supply wailing out into the desolate night of Ganymede.

At least it had been a quick death, with no time for the man to languish in a prison somewhere and eternally curse the day Kennedy had come to Ganymede.

He stopped by a wide-stretching lake whose "waters" glittered in the light of three whirling moons. Only they and vast Jupiter seemed to be watching as Kennedy gently lifted Engel's oddly light body from the sled and carried it to where the dark liquid lapped the edge of the ragged shore.

He waded out a foot or two into the lake and laid Engel face-down on the surface of the water. He drifted. Kennedy touched one gauntlet to the dead man's boot and shoved, imparting enough force to send Engel floating slowly but inexorably out toward the middle of the lake.

To Kennedy's horror the body remained afloat for some minutes, spinning in a lazy circle as the currents of the lake played games with it. Face down, arms and legs hovering on the crest of the lake, Engel looked like an effigy, a straw dummy put out to drift. But finally the methane came bubbling in through the two holes in his breathing-helmet, and the spacesuit lost its buoyancy and grew heavy, filling with liquid until Engel slowly and gravely vanished beneath the surface.

Kennedy remained there a moment in tribute. He had not known Engel at all; in the words of the Ganny poem, he was only a shadow of a man to Kennedy. The linguist had been a man without a past to him, just a face and a name and an ability to collect words and understand their meaning. Kennedy had not known how old Engel was,

97

where he had been born or educated, whether or not he was married, where he lived when he was on Earth, what his hopes or aspirations were, his philosophy of life. And now no one of those things mattered. Engel had neither present nor future, and his past was irrelevant.

Kennedy remounted the sled and continued on. The time was 0412; he would reach the village at about 0445, and according to his schedule that was the time at which the Gannys would begin to stir into wakefulness after their last period of sleep. He rode silently on, not thinking, not making any plans.

He was still a mile from the village when he saw the Terran truck from the outpost, drawn up perhaps fifty or a hundred yards from the first houses of the village. He looked down on the scene from the row of razor-backed ridges that bordered the village on the south. When he was close enough, he could see clearly what was taking place.

The villagers were lined up outside their houses, and four dark spacesuited figures moved among them. An interrogation was under way. They were questioning the villagers about Engel and himself, hoping to find out where they were hiding.

As Kennedy watched, one of the spacesuited figures knocked a villager to the ground. The Ganny rose and stood patiently where he had stood before. Brutally the Earthman knocked him down again.

Kennedy's jaws tightened. Gunther was prepared to stop at nothing in the attempt to find him. Maybe he would move on to wholesale destruction of the village, when no information was forthcoming.

With his chin he nudged the control of his suit-microphone and said, "Gunther?"

"Who's that?"

"Kennedy. Hold your fire."

"Where are you, Kennedy?"

"On the hill overlooking you. Don't fire. I don't intend to make trouble."

He had no choice. He could not hide out on this frozen methane world for long, and the aliens, though they meant well, could not give him shelter, could not feed him. He would only be bringing pain and suffering to them if he tried to remain at large.

"What are you doing up there?" Gunther asked.

"I'm coming down. I'm surrendering. I don't want to cause any more suffering. Got that? I'm surrendering. I'll come down out of the hills with my hands up. Don't hurt the villagers any more. They aren't to blame."

He rose from the shed and slowly made his way down the side of the hill, a dark figure against the whiteness. He was no more than halfway down when Gunther's voice said sharply, "Wait a minute! You're alone. Where's Engel? If this is some sort of trick—"

"Engel's dead. You killed him back at the airlock when we escaped, and I gave him burial in a lake back beyond the hills. I'm coming down alone. Hold your fire, Gunther."

14

THE CORPORATION spaceship had not been intended as a prison ship, and so they had no facilities for confining him. Not that Kennedy was anxious to mingle with the men of the crew; reserved, aloof, a little shocked despite himself at the magnitude of what he had done, he rarely left the hammock during the long, tense trip back to Earth. He spent much of his time reading and as much as possible sleeping, or thinking about the Ganymedean culture of which he had had such a brief, tantalizing glimpse.

He ate alone, and spoke to the other men aboard the ship only when necessary. They spoke to him not at all.

The last few days before the departure of the supply ship had been unpleasant ones. Gunther had ordered Kennedy confined to the bare little dungeon-storeroom, with a guard constantly posted outside the door and meals brought in.

Gunther had questioned him.

"You're accused on two counts. You gave weapons to the aliens and you murdered Engel. Right?"

"I decline to answer that."

"The hell with that. Confess."

"I'm not confessing to hogwash like that. And don't threaten to have me shot, Gunther. The agency knows I'm here."

"It could be an accident—a man cleaning his rifle. But I won't do it. Let the Corporation take care of you. You're not my responsibility. You go back to Earth when the ship leaves."

"As you please," Kennedy said.

"But I want a confession. Tell me why you gave guns to the Gannys!"

"I didn't. The Gannys wouldn't know how to use them. And you killed Engel yourself, when we tried to get away."

"Who'll believe that? Come on, Kennedy—confess."

Kennedy shrugged and refused. After a while, Gunther gave up.

He had to admit to himself they were taking special care of him. Another man might have killed him on the spot, as a safety measure; Gunther was too smart for that. After all, Kennedy was an agency executive. This was too big a thing for Gunther to handle, and he knew it. He was tossing it back to the Corporation, letting them judge Kennedy and decide what to do with him.

Sizer let him have a gravanol pill on the way out, which surprised him a little; it was reasonable to expect that they'd leave a traitor to cope with the agonies of blast-off acceleration as best he could, without proffering the assistance of the pain-killing drug. They gave it to him, though, silently and ungraciously, but readily enough.

He had never been a particularly thoughtful man. Intelligent, yes; quick-witted, yes; resourceful, yes. But *thinking* —evaluation of himself in relation to the world about him, understanding of the sea of events through which he moved—thinking had never been his strong point, as Marge had so frequently let him know. But now he had plenty of time to think, as the Corporation ship left the icy ball that was Ganymede far behind and coasted on toward Earth.

They had taught him many things at Northwestern; he

100

had responded to tutorial prodding magnificently, coming through with straight A averages for the entire four years. But no one had ever taught him where his loyalties belonged. And he had never bothered to find out.

It was a world he had never made—but one that had given him thirty thousand a year at the biggest public relations firm there was, and he'd been content. He could have left well enough alone, he thought.

The day of Earthfall came. Word passed rapidly through the ship, and Sizer, grim-faced now, with none of the cheerful affability of the earlier journey, came aft to offer Kennedy a gravanol pill. He accepted the pellet and the flask and nodded his thanks to Sizer. The Spaceman left.

Kennedy looked carefully around, making sure no one was watching him. A wild plan was forming in his mind. He palmed the little pill and drained the flask of water; then he slumped back in the hammock as if drugged. He slipped the pill into his pocket.

Deceleration began.

He rode down into the atmospheric blanket fully conscious, the only man on the ship who was awake. The ship's jets thundered, stabilizing her, decelerating her. Kennedy felt as if two broad hands were squeezing him together, jamming his neck against his spine, flattening his face, distorting his mouth. He could hear the currents of blood in his body. He gasped for breath like a hooked fish. It seemed that there was a mighty knuckle pressing against his chest, expelling the air from his lungs, keeping him from drawing breath.

He drew a breath. And another.

He swung in the cradle. Waves of pain shivered through him.

He started to blank out. He fought it, clinging tightly to consciousness.

And he stayed awake.

The ship was trembling, shuddering in the last moments before landing. He did not look out the viewplate, but he knew the ground must be visible now, pitching wildly beneath the ship. He could picture the sleek vessel standing perched on a tongue of fire.

They dropped down. Kennedy wiped a trickle of blood from his upper lip. He became abruptly aware of a roaring silence, and realized that the bellow of the jets had at last ceased.

They had landed. And he had not blanked out.

Now he rolled over and looked through the port as he began to unfasten himself. He saw people out there. A welcoming committee? He looked for Marge or Watsinski or Spalding, but saw no one he recognized, no familiar face. He blinked again, realizing the field was empty. Those were just maintenance men. The ship had returned under wraps of secrecy.

What a blaster of a dream that was, he thought, and in the same moment he realized that it was no dream. He had spent three weeks on another world; he had discovered that the values he held to be true were false, and that the cause he had lent himself to was dedicated to wiping out a culture that had incredibly much to offer Earth. The Corporation did not hate the Gannys. They merely stood in the way of making profit, and so they had to go.

A voice said quietly inside him, *If you run fast enough they can't touch you. It's not too late. You didn't commit any crime by talking to the Gannys. The Corporation hasn't started making the law yet, dammit. Not yet.*

The big hatch in the wall of the ship was opening, and a catwalk was extruding itself automatically so the men in the ship could reach the ground twenty feet below. Very carefully Kennedy unlaced the webbing that held him in the deceleration cradle. He dropped one foot over the side of the hammock, then the other, and went pitching forward suddenly as the wall of the ship came sweeping up to meet him.

He thrust out his hands desperately, slapped them against the wall, steadied himself. He waited a moment until his head stopped pounding and his feet were less rubbery. He glanced fore and saw the other crewmen still slumped in their cradles, groggy from the gravanol pills. It would be a few minutes yet before they awakened. And they never would have expected their prisoner to have risked, and made, a fully conscious landing.

Kennedy smiled. Quite calmly he made his way forward to the hatch and lowered himself down the catwalk to the ground. Someone in the ship yawned; they were beginning to stir.

The sun was warm and bright. He had forgotten the

day, but he knew it would have to be somewhere near the end of July. The sickly heat of midsummer hung over the flat grounds of the landing field.

A few maintenance men were moving toward the ship now, but they ignored him. Somehow he had expected welcomers, video cameras, a galaxy of flash bulbs—not an empty field. But the Corporation had probably preferred a veil of secrecy cast over the arrival.

He made his way across the field and into the area beyond. He spied a taxi passing on the road and hailed it. He felt dazed by the heat after the chill of Ganymede, and the punishment of landing had left him wobbly.

He opened the taxi and slipped into the passenger's seat. He glanced out the window and looked back at the space-field. By now they were awake aboard the ship, and knew he was missing.

"Step on it, driver. Take me to the city."

The cab rolled away. Kennedy wondered if he would be followed. It had been so simple to slip away, in the confusion of landing. One of the Ganny maxims he had learned was that through endurance of pain comes knowledge of truth, and therefore freedom. Well, he had endured pain and he had his freedom as a result of it. The unused gravanol pill was still in his pocket.

He had slipped away from them. Like in a dream, he thought, where the figures reach out to clutch you but you slip through them like a red-hot blade through butter.

They would hunt him, of course. Escape could never be this simple; the Corporation would spare no expense to get him and put him away. But if he only had a few days of freedom to accomplish some of the things he had to do, he would be content. Otherwise his surrender would have been pointless; he might just as well have spent his days as a fugitive on Ganymede.

Where can I go? he wondered.

Home?

Home was the most obvious place. So obvious, in fact, that his pursuers might never suspect he would go there. Yes. Home was best. He gave the cabby the address and lapsed back into sullen somnolence for the rest of the trip.

The house looked unusually quiet, he thought, as the cab pulled into the Connecticut township where he and Marge had lived so long.

Maybe Gunther had radioed ahead. Maybe they had intentionally let him slip away at the spaceport, knowing that they could always pick him up at home.

He gave the driver much too big a bill and without waiting for change headed up the drive into his garden.

He found his key in his trouser pocket, pressed it into the slot, and held his right thumb against the upper thumb-plate until the front door slid back. He stepped inside.

"Marge?"

No answer. He half-expected an answering rattle of gunfire or the sudden appearance of the Corporation gendarmerie, but the house remained silent. Only the steady purr of the electronic dust-eater was audible. He went on into the living room, hoping at least to find the cat sleeping in the big armchair, but there was no cat. Everything was tidy and in its place. The windows were opaqued.

The windows were opaqued! Kennedy felt a twinge of shock. They never opaqued the windows except when they expected to be away for long periods of time, on vacations, long shopping tours. Marge would never have left the windows opaqued in the middle of the day like that—

Suspicion began to form. He saw a piece of paper sitting on the coffee-table in the living room. He picked it up.

It was a note, in Marge's handwriting, but more shaky than usual. All it said was, *Ted, there's a tape on the recorder. Please listen to it, Marge.*

His hands trembled slightly as he switched on the sound system and activated the tape recorder. He waited a moment for the sound to begin.

"Ted, this is Marge speaking to you—for what's going to be the last time. I was going to put this in the form of a note, but I thought using the recorder would let me make things a little clearer.

"Ted, I'm leaving. It's not a hasty step. I thought about it a long time, and when this Ganymede business came up everything seemed to crystallize. We just shouldn't be living together. Oh, it was nice at times—don't get me wrong. But there's such a fundamental difference in our outlook toward things that a break had to be made—now, before it was too late to make it.

"You worked on the Ganymede thing casually, light-
104

heartedly, and didn't even realize that I was bitterly opposed to it. Things like that. I'm not leaving because of a difference in politics, or anything else. Let's just say that the Ganymede job was a symptom, not a cause, of the trouble in our marriage. I hated the contract and what it stood for. You didn't even bother to examine the meaning of it. So today—the day you left for space, Ted—I'm leaving.

"I'm going away with Dave Spalding. Don't jump to conclusions, though—I wasn't cheating on you with Dave. I have my code and I live by it. But we did discuss the idea of going away together, and your leaving for Ganymede has made it possible. That's why I wanted you to go. Please don't be hurt by all this—please don't smash things up and curse. Play the tape a couple of times, and *think* about things. I don't want anything that's in the house; I took what I wanted to keep, the rest is yours. After you've had time to get used to everything I'll get in touch with you about the divorce.

"So that's it, Ted. It was grand while it lasted, but I knew it couldn't *stay* grand much longer, and to spare both of us fifty or sixty years of bitterness, I've pulled out. Dave has left the agency, but we have a little money that we've both saved. Again, Ted, I'm sorry, sorry for both of us.

"I left the cat with the Camerons, and you can get him back from them when you get back from Ganymede. Nobody but you and Dave and me knows what's happened. Take care of yourself, Ted. And so long."

He let the tape run down to the end and shut it off. Then he stood numbly in the middle of the room for a long while, and after that he played the tape over once again from the beginning to end.

Marge. Dave Spalding. And the cat was with the Camerons.

"I didn't expect that, Marge," he said quietly. His throat felt very dry. His eyes ached; but he did not cry at all.

15

HE POURED himself a drink, and even that was not without its painful contingent memories, because Marge had always poured his drinks for him. Then he took off his shoes and listened to the tape a third time, with much the same frame of mind as the man who keeps hitting his head against a brick wall because it feels so good when he stops.

This time around he was able to stop hearing Marge's words and listen to the way she was saying them: straightforwardly, with little hesitation or emotional quaver. These were words she had stored within her a long time, he realized, and she seemed almost happy to relieve herself of them.

No, he thought, he hadn't expected Marge to do something like this; and that, perhaps, was why she had done it. She was mercurial, unpredictable. He saw now he had never really known her at all.

Some minutes passed, and the first rough shock ebbed away. He looked at it almost philosophically now. It had been inevitable. She had acted with great strength and wisdom. The Ted Kennedy who had been to Ganymede and had his eyes opened there respected her for it.

But he felt bitterness at the fact that he had returned from Ganymede a changed man, a man who had not only shifted his stand but who had taken positive action in his new allegiance, and Marge was not here to commend him for having seen her point of view at last. His conversion had come too late for that. There was no point chasing after her, finding her, saying, "Look, Marge, I've finally repudiated the Corporation and the agency—won't you come back now?"

No. It was too late to wave his new-found allegiance and expect Marge to forgive all his old blunders. Half the unhappiness people make for each other, he thought, is caused by men and women trying to put back together something that should remain forever smashed.

It hurt, but he forced himself to forget her.

He rose, crossed the room and snapped on the video. He searched for a newscast and finally found one on Channel Seventy-two, the Bridgeport UHF channel. He listened patiently through the usual guff about the miserable late-July weather, hot and humid despite the best efforts of the Bureau of Weather Adjustment, and to an analysis of the new cabinet crisis in Yugoslavia. Then the newscaster paused, as if turning over a sheet of script, and said, "Spacefield Seven in New Jersey was the scene several hours ago of the arrival from Ganymede of Captain Louis Hills' space ferry, which had made its last trip to Ganymede three weeks ago laden with supplies for the colony there. Captain Hills reported all well on the tiny world. In an afternoon baseball game, the Red Sox defeated the—"

Kennedy moved to shut the set off. They had decided to suppress all news of him, then—and they were still rigorously maintaining the fiction that Ganymede was populated by brave men and women from Earth. Well, that was no surprise. There would be an intensive man hunt for him as soon as the Corporation could mobilize its forces. Perhaps it was already under way.

Kennedy started to form his plans. Today was July 30. The Corporation planned to go before the United Nations and ask for armed intervention on October 11. He had until then to secure evidence that would puncture the fabric of lies he had helped erect.

But he would have to move warily. The Corporation would be looking for him, anxious to shut him up before he could damage the project. And before long they would have the U.N. Security Police on his trail too, on the hoked-up grounds that he had given arms to the Ganymedeans and murdered Engel. He would have to run, run fast, and hide well. With both Corporation goons and official world police on his trail, he would need to be agile.

The phone rang. He had no idea who it might be. Marge, maybe. It didn't matter. If he answered, he might be putting the Corporation on his trail. He forced himself to let it ring, and after a while it stopped. He stared at the chocolate-colored receiver, wondering who might have called.

Well, it didn't matter.

He knew what he had to do: get incriminating data on the Ganymede hoax from the agency files, and turn it over to the U.N. But it wasn't as simple as that. Probably the instant he set foot in the agency building he'd be grabbed and turned over to the authorities, and from then on he'd never get a chance to speak up.

Of course, maybe the agency didn't know about his changed beliefs yet. Perhaps the Corporation had not seen fit to let Gunther's report get into agency hands yet; maybe Bullard and his cohorts intended to make a full loyalty investigation of the agency they had employed before letting Dinoli know that one of his hand-picked men had turned renegade on Ganymede.

But he couldn't take that risk. He would have to get the material out of the agency files by stealth, and somehow get it to a U.N. representative.

He would have to drop out of sight for a while. There was no hurry about the exposure; he had more than two months. If he hid somewhere for those two months and raided the agency when they least expected it—

He knew where he could hide. At his brother's place in Wisconsin.

Cautiously, he depolarized the windows and peered out of each, one by one, to make sure no one lurked outside. Then he opaqued them all again. He packed a single suitcase, taking with him just one change of clothes and a few toilet articles; this was no time to be burdened by personal property. He left everything else as it was—the bar, the kitchen, the living room with Marge's picture in it. He hoped the cat would be safe with the Camerons. He had had the cat for many years; he would miss it.

The phone rang again. He ignored it.

It stopped eventually. He waited just a moment, gathering his strength, and took a last quick look at the house he and Marge had picked together eight years before, and which he might never see again.

He was leaving the past behind. Marge, the cat, his bar, his collection of records, his books. All the things he had treasured. The solid, secure life for which he had long been smugly thankful, gone overnight. *Ted Kennedy, fugitive*. All his thirty-two years had been building toward this, and it seemed strange to him that such a destiny should have been at the end of the string of years that had unrolled for him thus far.

Good-bye, agency. Good-bye, books and records and drinks and wife, and sleepy old cat and exclusive Connecticut township. *Addio*. He had few regrets. His brief contact with the Gannys had taught him to put less value on material things than he once had; he was calmer, more purposeful, since learning from them. Which was why he was giving up everything in an attempt to save the Ganymedeans.

He saw that their culture had to be preserved—and that he alone could save them.

There was a gun in his night-table drawer, a snub-nosed .38 Marge had made him buy three years before, when a night prowler had terrified the females of the area. He had never used it. Fully loaded, it had rested in the drawer.

Now he slipped it into its shoulder holster and donned it, scowling in annoyance because he would need to wear a jacket in the July heat to conceal the gun. The weapons permit was somewhere in the drawer; he rummaged for it, found it finally, and slipped it into his suitcase.

The time was 1632. Kennedy thought a moment: *they may be monitoring my phone, so it isn't safe to phone the airline from here. I'll go into town to make my reservations.*

He opened the front door and cautiously looked around. No one was in sight. Either they hadn't traced him to his home yet, or they were going to let him run a little before coming down hard.

He locked the door behind him and went around back to the garage. He put his luggage in the trunk compartment, got into the car, and drove down onto the main road without looking back.

Ten minutes later he was in town. "Town" consisted of two or three stores, a bank, a post office, a church. It probably had not changed much in the past century; small towns always resist change longer than large cities. Kennedy drove down the county road into the main square and parked near the clock, which was a big old one that had been standing in the center of the town well over a century, and of course still used the twelve-hour system. He glanced up at it, frowning a bit as he computed the time. The hands read 4:45, which he translated back into the more familiar 1645. Less than three hours had passed since his landing at Spacefield Seven.

It was an hour at which the town was quiet. The afternoon movie show still had ten or fifteen minutes to run; those who weren't at it were home waiting for dinner.

Kennedy left his parked car and stepped into Schiller's, the combined pharmacy-newsstand-luncheonette-department store that served the township. Two or three locals were sipping sodas at the fountain as he came in. Kennedy scooped change from his pocket and found he had no telephone tokens. The phone in Schiller's did not have an automatic vending machine in the booth, either.

He put a quarter on the counter and said, "Give me two phone tokens, please."

"Sure. Oh, hello there, Mr. Kennedy." Schiller looked at him speculatively a moment. He was a man in his sixties or seventies, old enough certainly to remember well back into the last century; his eyes were still clear blue, his hair only recently had gone white. He wiped his hands on his stained white smock and said, "Couple of men were in here just a minute ago asking for you. Wanted to know which road to take to get out to your place, so I had my boy show them. Must have been friends of yours."

"I'm not expecting any," Kennedy said. He took the tokens from the counter.

"Hey, there they are!" Schiller exclaimed, pointing.

Through the plate-glass front window, Kennedy saw two men in dark brown business suits and austere violet traveling cloaks coming out of the bank. They were grim, efficient-looking men. Corporation men, Kennedy thought. He started to walk quickly toward the telephone booths in the rear of the store.

"Hey, Mr. Kennedy," Schiller called. "You better go out there and see those fellers before they get into their car and go chasin' all the way out to your place."

"I don't have time to see them. I've got to get into the city on some important business."

"You want me to go out there and tell 'em that?" Schiller asked helpfully.

110

"No—that'll only offend them. Let them make an appointment with me next time they want to see me at home." He ducked into the telephone booth in time to cut off one of Schiller's stale monologues on the ways of the new generation, and how they charged around so fast they never had time to talk to each other.

Kennedy asked for Information, got the number of the ticket deck at Roosevelt Airport, and was told that the next flight for Milwaukee was departing at 1951 that evening, arrival time in Milwaukee 2113 Milwaukee time. That sounded fine to Kennedy.

"Make a reservation for *one*," he said. "The name is Engel." He gave the name almost unthinkingly, automatically.

"First name, please?" came the impersonal reply.

"Ah—Victor. Victor Engel."

"Thank you, sir. Would you please pick up your reservation no later than an hour before departure time?"

"I'll do that," Kennedy said. He hung up, listened to his token click down into the depths of the phone, and left the booth.

Schiller said, "Just like I told you, Mr. Kennedy. Those friends of yours drove off toward your place while you were on the phone. Guess they're going to waste some time now."

"I guess so," Kennedy said. He grinned. "I just didn't have time to see them, though. I have to get down to the city in a hurry. My boat leaves at 1900."

"Boat?"

Kennedy nodded. "I'm going to Europe for a month on company business. Don't tell a soul, of course. I really don't want it getting around or all my friends will expect me to bring back souvenirs."

He waved genially and left. As he drove rapidly down the Thruway toward New York, he thought about Schiller and the two bleak-faced Corporation men. They were certain to come back to town once they found his house empty; perhaps they would stop in at Schiller's again, and in that case they were certain to get drawn into conversation with the old man.

He hoped they had a nice time looking for him on the departing boats to Europe.

16

He drove down into New York City, cutting left on the Thruway and taking the artery that led out along the south shore of Long Island Sound to the big new airport. Roosevelt Airport was a city in itself, practically; its rambling acres covered a great chunk of Long Island. It served as the airline capital of the world.

Kennedy reached the parking area at 1747 and turned his car over to the attendant.

"Want her shined up, sir? Refueled, overhauled?"

Kennedy shook his head. "Sorry, thanks."

"Those deflectors look like they could use—"

"No," Kennedy said. He took the parking ticket, which had the time stamped on it, and folded it away in his wallet. The attendant was going to be surprised when no one ever showed up to claim the dented '42 Frontenac.

He made his way toward the shining plastic building that housed the central ticket offices and got on a line that moved slowly toward a window labelled *Reservations For Today's Flights.*

When he reached the window he gave his name: "Victor Engel. I'm going to Milwaukee."

"Of course, Mr. Engel." The girl performed three quick motions with her hands and slid a crisp white folder under the grill toward him.

"One hundred thirteen fifty," she said.

Kennedy took two bills from his wallet, passed them over and received his change. Normally he would have paid by check—but the reservation was in Engel's name, and he would have had to sign the check that way. There would have been immediate catastrophe. It was impossible to pass a bad check when the lightning-fast receptors of the

112

Central Clearing House in Chicago could check his signature against their files and report back within fifteen seconds.

It was too bad he had to buy round-trip tickets, too. The return half would expire in thirty days, and he had no intention of returning East so soon. But a one-way trip might arouse suspicion, and he wanted to keep Victor Engel as free of suspicion as possible.

Victor Engel. The first name had been a sudden guess. It had been a curious moment when he realized he had never known the dead linguist's first name.

He moved out of the ticket deck onto the promenade. In the distance, outlined against the setting sun, a huge plane was coming in—one of the FB-11 stratoliners, the five-hunded-passenger jet jobs that crossed the country from New York to California in just under two hours. He watched it taxi in, like a great bird returning to its nest.

He ate alone in an automatic restaurant—a light meal, protoid sandwich and milk, for he was far from hungry just now—and bought an evening 'fax-sheet at a vending stand. Quickly, he made his way past the West Coast baseball scores, past the usual item on the weather, past the latest on the Yugoslavian ministerial shake-up. He found a squib on the return of the Ganymede ship. There was no mention of the public relations man who had fled the spacefield hotly pursued by Corporation mobsters.

He crumpled the 'fax-sheet and dumped it in a disposal. Finding himself outside a bookstore, he went in, browsed for half an hour, and emerged with a couple of paperbacks.

He strolled the promenade as the heat of the day died away, waiting for departure time. At 1925 the announcement came, "Universal Airlines plane for Milwaukee, Flight 165, now loading passengers at Gate 17."

The ship was not the newest model—an FB-9, seating ninety, a fairly low-ceiling liner that never went higher than 20,000 feet on passenger flights. As he boarded it, the stewardess, a shy-looking, rosy-cheeked blonde, smiled and said, "Good evening, Mr. Engel. I hope you have a pleasant flight."

"Thank you," he said, and found a seat in the front, to the fore of the wings.

113

After spaceflight, airplane flying seemed odd to Kennedy—oddly clumsy and oddly unsafe. The plane took off on schedule, roaring down the runway and veering sharply upward into the sky; he looked down at the darkening streets of Brooklyn and saw tiny dots that were autos passing below, and then Brooklyn passed out of sight as the ship stabilized at its flight altitude of 20,000 feet.

At that height they were well above the clouds, which formed a solid gray-white floor stretching to the horizon, billowing up here and there in puffs that looked like ice floes on a frozen sea. There was little sensation of vibration or of motion, but at no time was Kennedy deceived into believing that the plane was not moving, as so often he had felt aboard the spaceship.

He read for a while, but lost interest quickly and dozed off. Sooner than he expected, they were in Milwaukee; his watch read 2213, but he jabbed the setting stud to put the hands back an hour, to conform with local time.

The Milwaukee airport probably had been a local wonder a century before; now, it merely looked cheap and shabby, a weathered old edifice of green glass and plastic. Kennedy treated himself to a cup of synthetic caffeine drink in one of the airport restaurants, and considered his next several steps.

It was an hour's drive from Milwaukee to Brockhurst, where he had been born and where his older brother still lived. But it was late, and he felt hesitant about barging in on them unannounced when he knew he could not get out there much before midnight. Steve had always been a man of regular habits, and though he probably wouldn't say anything if his brother arrived unexpectedly near midnight, it would upset his routine.

Instead of going out there, Kennedy took a cab to town and rented a room in the first hotel he found. In the morning he dialed his brother's number as soon as he was up, at 0800. Steve would be having breakfast about that time, before going out on the day's run.

He was right. A gruff deep voice said, "Kennedy speaking. Who's this?"

"Kennedy, this is Kennedy. Of the Connecticut Kennedys, you know."

A moment of silence. Then: "Ted?"

"None other."

Hesitantly: "What—what's on your mind?"

"I thought I'd come visit you," Kennedy said. "I got into Milwaukee last night, too late to call."

"Oh. I see."

That wasn't like his brother at all; Steve normally would have been effusively cordial. Now he sounded worried and tense.

"Look, Steve, I'll take the next bus out to your place. I'm here alone, and I can't explain everything over the phone. Can you wait till I get there? I'll—"

"No," Steve said bluntly. "Stay in Milwaukee. I'll come see you. Where are you?"

"Hotel Avon. But—"

"You stay there. I'll be there in an hour."

Puzzled, Kennedy hung up. He didn't understand. Steve always had an invitation ready for him. But now, when he needed him, Steve seemed unwilling.

Maybe, he thought, Steve was getting even. He knew he had neglected Steve for a long time, and maybe now Steve resented it. But the only thing he and Steve had ever had in common was a set of parents.

Steve was eleven years his senior, and, since their father had died when Ted was seven, had served as head of the family. Steve was the salt-of-the-earth type, the hearty middle-western sort, big-bodied and smiling, with a fondness for beer and fishing excursions. He was a faithful churchgoer. He had quarreled endlessly with his brother, until Ted, more nervous by temperament, introverted and intellectual, had left home after high school, gone to Chicago and enrolled in Northwestern.

The brothers had met just once since Kennedy's marriage to Marge—in 2039, when a vacation trip of Steve's had brought him East. It had been an awkward meeting; Steve and his plump wife Betty had been ill at ease in the modern surroundings of the Kennedy home. The music he played for them had bored them, the books had awed them, and once Betty had hit a raw nerve by asking Marge when she expected to start raising a family. Betty had had two children already, with a third on the way. Marge had blushed and tried to explain that it wasn't because they didn't *want* children that they didn't have any. Since that time, Kennedy had exchanged letters with his brother sporadically, but as the years passed they had had

115

less and less to say to each other. It was nearly ten months since he had last written to Steve.

Now he waited, pacing tensely around the confines of the shabby Milwaukee hotel room. Shortly after 0900, Steve arrived.

He had grown gray, Kennedy noticed, but he still looked impressive, a big-muscled, thick-bodied man with deep, sad eyes that belied the essentially untroubled mind behind them. He squeezed Kennedy's right hand mercilessly. Next to his brother, Kennedy felt suddenly shamefaced; he was Easternized, high-strung, overintellectual, and probably looked a woeful figure to his healthy, happy brother.

"I want to apologize," Steve said huskily. "I couldn't let you come out to the house."

"Why not?"

Steve flicked his eyes uncertainly around the room. "Are you in some kind of trouble, Ted?"

"Not really."

"I can always tell when you lie to me. You just lied. Ted, I was always afraid you'd get mixed up in something bad. I tried to teach you to do your day's work and leave well enough alone, but I guess it never really took, or else the people down East taught you different. What did you do, Ted?"

"I didn't do anything," Kennedy lied. "I just want to stay at the house, quietly, for a while."

"You can't do that."

Coming from Steve, that was flatly incredible. "Why?"

Steve sighed. "I got a call last night from the local Security people. They wanted to know if I was your brother. I said yes. They said you were in big trouble back East, and you were wanted by Security. They wouldn't tell me what for. Then they said I'd have to cooperate or I'd be subject to arrest as an accessory after the fact."

Kennedy felt cold despite the blistering heat. "What else did they say?"

"They said you were missing and were likely to try to come to me. That if you came out here I was to notify them immediately, or else they'd make it hard on me. Then they asked me for a list of any other relatives of ours anywhere in the country, and I guess I gave it to them. Then they hung up. Ted, what have you done?"

Kennedy gripped his brother's thick arm tightly. "I swear to you I haven't done anything wrong. I've been framed by a bunch of criminals, and I have to hide for a while. I want to stay here with you."

"That's what they said you'd want to do. Sorry, Ted. You can't."

"*Can't?*"

Steve shook his head. "I've got a wife and five kids, Ted. A place in the community. I can't risk losing all that. They told me I could go to prison for twenty years if I helped you."

"It's a lie!"

"Be that as it may. You better go somewhere else." Steve fished into his pocket. "I brought you some money. I guess you need it. Don't argue; just take it."

He pushed a thousand dollars in small bills into Kennedy's nerveless fingers.

"I better go now," Steve said. "Maybe they followed me. If they catch you, don't tell 'em you saw me at all. Or spoke to me." Beads of sweat dribbled down Steve's heavy face; he looked close to tears. "I'm sorry about this, kid. But I have to think of my family first. You understand?"

"Yeah, Steve. I understand."

17

KENNEDY waited fifteen minutes after his brother left, went downstairs, and checked out. He knew the chase was on, now. They had called his brother. Probably they had called anyone in the hemisphere who knew him at all, and bullied them into refusing to give him aid.

He was on his own, now. And he would have to run.

Now that the hunt had begun, time was against him. He had to secure his evidence and present it to the U.N., and he had to do it before his pursuers found him. But how, when he was sought by the Corporation and the U.N.? He had no answer. But he knew doggedly he was going to try. He summoned up as much as he could remember of the Ganny poetry—the didactic philosophical poems on survival in a hostile environment. The Gannys knew what suffering meant. And they were tough, those peaceful, violence-hating aliens. Tougher than any Earthman.

It was dangerous for him to return to New York by any direct route. He decided to go overland, by bus perhaps, taking several weeks to do it. He let a mustache grow, and before he left Milwaukee he visited a barber; his long agency haircut gave way to a midwestern trim that left the back of his neck and his ears bare. That would make him just a little harder to recognize.

He discovered, with a little shock, that Watsinski, or whoever it was that was continuing the Ganymede colony hoax, had worked him into the framework.

He was wanted, said the telefaxes and newssheets, for having distributed arms to the Gannys. According to the 'fax he picked up in Chicago three days after leaving Milwaukee, he had been sent to Ganymede to do a series of magazine articles on the colony, but instead had treacherously murdered a member of the colony and had given ammunition to the aliens. Then, being sent back to Earth under arrest, he had escaped and was being sought for treason against humanity, with a fat reward for his capture.

He stared at the picture of himself in the telefax. It was an old shot, taken when he was twenty pounds heavier, wore his hair long, and had no mustache. The sleek, complacent face on the shiny yellow sheet bore little resemblance to his own.

He headed East, keeping himself inconspicuous and crossing streets to avoid Security men. He tried not to get into conversations with strangers. He kept to himself. He was the needle in the haystack of 225,000,000 people, and if he was lucky they might not find him.

As he moved on, he kept in touch with the news from Ganymede. The character of the bulletins had taken on a distinct new coloration.

Now there was word of sinister alien armies marching beyond the hills, of bomb detonations and the dry sound of target practice. "The aliens are becoming very resentful of our presence," wrote Colony Director Lester Brookman in the syndicated column that appeared in the nation's papers on August 11. "Undoubtedly they have been stirred up by the traitor Theodore Kennedy, who, I understand, is still at large on Earth. They object to our presence on their world and have several times made ugly threats. During the current crisis we do not permit members of the colony to leave the dome in groups of less than three."

It was proceeding according to plan, Kennedy thought. The hostile aliens were on the warpath; soon they would be hunting for scalps; then would come the massacre. After that the troops would be called in to wipe out the belligerent savages. It was an old, old pattern of colonial expansion.

He knew the schedule. By September 17 the world would know that the colony of Earthmen was in imminent danger of being wiped out by the aliens, who refused to listen to reason and enter into peaceful negotiations. Five days of artful cliff-hanging would follow, and on September 22 the Corporation would make preliminary overtures toward the United Nations, asking for a police force to be sent to Ganymede to guard Terran interests. It would not be too strong a plea, for the public would need more manipulating. From September 22 through October 10 the world would pray for the endangered Earthmen; on October 11 the aliens would sweep down from the hills and virtually wipe out the gallant colony.

And, by October 17, United Nations troops would be on their way to Ganymede to quell the disturbance and police the world to make it safe for the Corporation.

Kennedy knew he had to act before October 11. After that, no amount of proof would seem convincing to a world determined to believe that a massacre had taken place.

But how could he get the evidence he needed?

He was in Trenton, New Jersey, eating lunch in a roadhouse, when the news came blaring forth: *Ganymede Colony Attacked!* The day was Sunday, September 17.

The cook reached over and turned up the radio behind the counter.

"A surprise alien attack shortly before dawn Ganymede time left the Earth colony on Jupiter's moon in grave peril

119

today," came the announcer's voice. "An estimated five thousand aliens, armed with clubs and native weapons, swept down on the dome that houses the colony, shouting 'Death to the Earthmen!' Colony Director Lester Brookman radioed later in the day that the assault had been beaten back, but only with the loss of three Earth lives and considerable damage to the colony.

"Names of the casualties and further developments will be brought to you as soon as they are released."

A pale, pasty-faced woman eating further up along the counter exclaimed, "How horrible! Those poor people, fighting against those savages!"

"Couple of fellows were talking today that maybe the U.N.'s going to send troops up there to keep everything peaceful," the cook said. "But they better hurry if they're going to do it, or there'll be a massacre."

Kennedy frowned tightly, saying nothing, and wolfed his food. He wanted to tell them that their fears were for nothing, that there was no colony up there, that this whole alien attack had sprung full-blown from a public relations agency's drawing board months before, and was neatly calculated to be revealed this day. That the fierce savages of Ganymede were actually wise and good and harmless people.

But he could not tell them these things.

He slipped into New York late that night and rented a room in Manhattan, in a dreary old slum of a hotel in the mid-sixties overlooking the East River. The name he gave was Victor Engel of Brockhurst, Wisconsin.

The hotel was populated by a curious sort of flotsam—desiccated leftovers from the last century, mostly, who remembered the days when Life Was Really Good. Kennedy, who had taken an intensive course in twentieth-century sociohistory as part of the requirements for his degree in Communications, smiled at the darkest era of the nerve-fraying Cold War of 1946–95, the five decades of agonizing psychological jousting that had led to the Maracaibo Pact and the lasting worldwide unity that had followed. It was as if the Depression of 1995 had wiped away their memories of childhood, taking away the threat of thermonuclear obliteration that had menaced these oldsters during their youth, leaving only a time-hazed remembrance of an Elysian era.

Well, that was their fantasy, Kennedy thought, and he would not puncture it. The Golden Age syndrome was a common accompaniment to senility, and at least they had the never-never world of their dreams to compensate for the bleakness of their declining days.

At least they had some form of happiness. *And what do I do now?* he asked himself.

He was in New York, but he was no closer to the solution of his problem than if he were still on Ganymede, or on Pluto. He had no access to the incriminating data on file at the agency. He could not simply publicly proclaim his accusations—who would believe the demented ravings of a murderer and a traitor? Time was growing short; in a few weeks, the attack would be made and the Gannys wiped out. And before long he would venture out on the street and be recognized, despite the changes he had made in his appearance.

On Wednesday he bought a newssheet and read it carefully. There was word from the beleaguered Ganymede colony, carefully fabricated by a Dinoli henchman. There was a notice to the effect that the traitor Theodore Kennedy was still at large, but that security authorities expected to apprehend him shortly.

And there was a little notice in the *Personals* column. Kennedy nearly overlooked it, but he read the column out of sheer boredom, hoping to find some diversion.

The notice said:

Dearest Ted, Will you forgive me? I realize now the mistake I made. Meet me at our home Thursday night and I will try to help you in what you are doing. Believe me, darling.

M.

He read it through five or six times. He wondered if it might be a Security trap. No; of course not. It *had* to be from Marge. She was the one person on this entire world that he could trust.

He decided to go to her.

18

THE HOUSE seemed to be sleeping; its windows were opaqued, its lawn overgrown and unkempt. Kennedy paid the cab driver and cautiously went up the walk to the door. The .38 was not far from his hand; he was ready in case Security men might be near.

He put his hand to the door, opened it, went in.

Marge was waiting in the living room for him.

She looked bad. She had aged, during the month; her face was pale and she had lost weight. Her hair looked stringy. Her lips were quivering; her face had no make-up on it, and her eyes were darting nervously around the room as Kennedy entered.

"Marge . . ."

"You saw the ad," she said in a harsh whisper. "I was praying you wouldn't. You never used to read that part of the paper."

"Praying I *wouldn't?* But—"

"Good evening, Ted," a male voice said. Dave Spalding stepped out of the kitchen. A tiny nickel-jacketed gun glinted in his hand.

"Spalding? But—"

"Please put your hands up, Ted. Marge, see if he has a gun."

Marge rose and walked unsteadily toward him. Her hands fumbled over him, quickly found the .38 in his pocket, and withdrew it. Silently she handed the gun to Spalding, who kept both of them covered during the procedure.

"I'm glad you didn't have any strange ideas about that gun, Marge," Spalding said levelly. There was just the hint of a quaver in his voice. "As I told you before, I can tell when you're getting ready to do something. You would have been dead five seconds before you pulled the trigger."

It irritated Kennedy to hear Spalding speaking this way in his own home. Leadenly he realized he had fallen into a trap with Marge as the bait.

He said, "What is this, Spalding?"

"Very simple. You're a very valuable piece of merchandise to me. I'm glad I got to you before Security did. I figured you might fall for something like this."

Kennedy looked at Marge in surprise. "I thought you two were simon-pure idealists. What's happening?"

"I left the agency shortly after your trip into space," Spalding said. "But it occurred to me recently that I might do better for myself if I returned. I phoned Dinoli and offered to find you—in exchange for a second-level position in the agency for myself."

Kennedy's eyes narrowed. "All the cynicism in the air finally made its impression on you, eh, Dave?" The callousness of the younger man's statements astonished him. "So you used Marge as bait and got me here, and now you'll sell me to Dinoli so you can get back into the agency you despised so much a few months ago. Very pretty, Dave."

Something like torment appeared on Spalding's face for a moment. Kennedy said nothing, staring at the gun in the other's hand.

He wasn't too surprised. He had always suspected that Spalding was a man of no real convictions, following the tide and struggling to find a safe port. He had found that port now. He had given up trying to swim upstream.

Spalding said, "I phoned Dinoli at home, as soon as I saw you coming into the house. Security men will be here soon. I just have to keep you here and wait for them, and I can have my second-level slot."

Kennedy glanced at Marge. "That was a splendid little speech you made on the recorder, Marge. All about how you were leaving me for Dave because Dave was true and good and virtuous and I was just an agency scoundrel. But I guess you see—"

"Shut up!" Spalding muttered.

"You've got the gun," Kennedy said. "If you don't like what I say, shoot me."

"No," Marge said. "Ted, he's gone crazy. Don't say things like that or he will shoot. He doesn't care."

Kennedy heard the clock ticking somewhere in the kitchen. He wondered how long it would take for the Security men to arrive. They would take him away, bury him somewhere in one of their interrogation centers, and the Ganymede invasion would go off as planned.

"Marge," Spalding said. "My throat's dry. Get me a drink of water from the kitchen."

She nodded and went inside. Kennedy smiled. "I'm disappointed," he said. "Not in you but in Marge. I thought she was a better judge of character than she turned out to be. She was really sold on you, I guess."

"I quit the agency, Kennedy. I tried to free-lance. I found out what it's like not to have money. I found out that having ethics isn't enough. They beat you down; they don't let you live. I couldn't fight them, so I made up my mind to join them again."

"Using me as the passkey," Kennedy said. "You knew that Dinoli and Bullard were combing the country for me, and that you had bait you could dangle, in the form of Marge. So you bargained with them. Well, good for you. I hope you're a success on second-level."

Marge returned from the kitchen, bearing a tall glass of water filled to the very top. "Here you are, Dave. It's ice-cold. Be careful you don't spill any. *Get him, Ted!*"

She hurled the water in Spalding's eyes and in the same motion threw herself against him, knocking his gun-hand to one side. Kennedy heard a roar and a boom and the thud of a slug burying itself in the wall, as he sprang toward the drenched, momentarily blinded Spalding.

He caught Spalding by the middle and spun him around. The gun waved wildly in the air. Kennedy grabbed for the gun-hand wrist, seized it and twisted, hoping to make him let go of the weapon. Instead, there was a second explosion.

Kennedy stepped back, startled by the vehemence of the blast. He felt no pain himself, and saw Marge's pale, frightened face. Spalding was sagging to the floor, a jagged hole in his throat and a bewildered, surprised look on his face.

Then Kennedy felt Marge against him. She was quivering, and he held her tight, trying to keep himself from

124

quivering also. He did not look at the dead man on the floor. He said quietly, "The gun went off while we were fighting. He shot himself. I think he's dead, Marge."

Through almost hysterical tears she said, "H-he put the ad in the paper. Then we came over here to wait for you. I tried to find some way of warning you, but there wasn't any. And now—"

A shudder ran through her, and through him as well. "I guess he deserved it," she said bleakly. "He would have turned you in. Ted, I've never seen a man get so rotten so fast. I was all wrong about him."

"You thought you loved him, didn't you?"

"Does it matter now?"

He tried to smile. "I guess not."

"You won't be bitter about it?"

Kennedy remembered fragments of a Ganny aphorism: *Forgiveness is the heart and soul of existence. The past must not bind the people of the present, for they must heed the nearness of the future.*

"We can start all over," he said, and for a few moments they said nothing. Then Kennedy abruptly broke away from her.

"Spalding said he called Security. They'll be here soon. I've got to get out of here."

"Where will you go?"

"Downtown, to the agency. I have to get together some evidence."

"What kind of—"

"I'll explain everything later. Do you have a car here?"

"It belonged to Dave. It's outside."

"Good. We have to get away from here, fast. And I have a job for you."

"Anything."

"I want you to get to see Harrison Flaherty—the chief American U.N. delegate." As he spoke, he removed the gun from Spalding's clenched hand, pocketed it, and restored his own to the shoulder holster. "I don't care how you manage it, but get in there to see him. Find out where he lives and see him at home—I know it's someplace in Manhattan. Tell him you're my wife, and that I'm coming over later to surrender myself to him in the name of the U.N."

"What—"

"Don't argue about it. Just do it. And let's get out of here now. I don't want them to catch me before I can give myself up."

They drove down into New York City, taking the Second Avenue Skyway, leaving Spalding sprawled in the living room for the Security men to find. Kennedy was wanted for one murder already; it made no difference if they tacked another to his dossier.

He drove off the Skyway at East 122nd Street and stopped in a store on the corner, where he checked the directomat and discovered that the U.N. man's residence was across town, at 89th Street overlooking the Hudson. He jotted down the address and pocketed it, and hailed a cab for Marge. The time was just before nine.

"I expect to be there in less than an hour," he told her. He slammed the cab door and it drove away. He started to walk.

The business district, at this hour of night, was utterly deserted. The wide streets were empty in a way Kennedy had never seen before. He turned up East 123rd to Lenox, and the office building that housed Steward and Dinoli was before him. He felt a nostalgic twinge. He looked around, and, seeing no watchman on duty, entered.

He passed through the open front door and was met immediately by an inner barrier. He had a key to it, but the key would work only if his thumbprint were registered in the building's central access file, down in the basement computer banks. It was a long chance, but removing a print from the computer banks was a troublesome business, and perhaps they had neglected to take his out.

He inserted his key and touched his thumb to the plate. The lock clicked; he pushed against the door and it swung back into its niche. They had not bothered to remove his thumbprint from the file after all.

He moved silently through the ghostly building, taking the stairs rather than the elevator (there was a concealed camera in the elevator that photographed all after-hours riders). Eight, nine, ten, eleven. Good old Floor Eleven again, after all these months. Almost three months. Last time he'd been here was the day before his ill-fated Ganymede journey. And now . . .

He used his key and his thumb again and let himself into

126

the office. The lights were off, the windows opaqued. The familiar steady hum of daytime agency activity was missing.

Quietly he made his way past the outer desk to his old cubicle. He clicked on the pocket flash he had found in the tool compartment of Spalding's car, and quickly gathered together the materials he wanted:

Dinoli's bulletin quoting the timetable for unfolding of the project.

The volume of characterizations of colonists he and Spalding had compiled.

Half a dozen damning inter-office memoranda.

His own master chart for developing crises in the day-to-day life of the Ganymede colonists.

It made a heavy little bundle. He shuffled it all together, found a big envelope and shoved it in. He had enough material here to explode the Ganymede hoax from top to bottom. The whole thing was here in all its cynical completeness.

He started to retrace his steps. He stopped; a light was on in one of the second-level offices in the back. Hastily, he shifted his burden from his left hand to the right and started to draw his gun.

A voice from behind him said, "What the hell do you think you're doing, Kennedy?"

He whirled suddenly and in the dimness he saw Ernie Watsinski, lean and stoop-shouldered, staring at him. The second-level man had evidently been working late this evening. He dodged behind a desk suddenly, and Kennedy saw that the executive had a gun.

Quickly, Kennedy flattened himself against a door and ducked into one of the fourth-level cubicles. He said crisply, "Throw down your gun, Ernie. I don't want to kill you. I've seen enough men dead on account of me."

"Suppose you throw down *your* gun," Watsinski replied. "I figured you'd come here eventually."

Kennedy leaned out as far as he dared. Watsinski was barely visible; Kennedy saw the edge of one long leg protrude from the side of a desk, then hurriedly draw back.

He heard the sound of a telephone dial being turned.

He heard Watsinski's voice: "Yes, give me Security. Hello? Ernest Watsinski speaking—of Steward and Dinoli. I'm in the S and D office now, and Ted Kennedy just attempted to break in. Eleventh floor. Yes, he's armed. So am I. We're in something of a stalemate right now. Get right over here."

The receiver dropped back into the cradle. Kennedy began to sweat. From trap to trap! He eyed the distant door and wondered if he dared make a break for it. He had no idea how good a shot Watsinski was, but he knew quite definitely that if he stayed here much longer he would be boxed in by Security.

He moistened his lips. "Ernie?"

"I'm here. Just sit tight, Kennedy. Security'll be here in a few minutes."

Calmly, Kennedy squeezed a shot out. The roar split the silence; he heard the sound of the bullet crashing harmlessly into the desk behind which Watsinski was hiding. The second-level man did not return the fire; the advantage was with him only so long as his gun held ammunition. Kennedy fired two more shots in quick succession. The first hit the wall behind Watsinski; Kennedy was hoping for a lucky ricochet. The second smashed into the lighting fixture above them.

The room went dark. Kennedy sprang to his feet and headed for the door, clutching his package desperately. He heard the sound of shots behind him, wild desperate shots fired by the angry Watsinski.

He grinned to himself as he ran down the eleven flights of stairs.

19

HE EMERGED breathless in front of the building and stopped for a moment. The drizzle that had been starting as he entered the building had developed into a full-sized autumn squall. Kennedy reflected that the Bureau of

Weather Adjustment had always been better at making rain than in heading it off.

The car was parked a block away. He started to run, wrapping his package under his jacket to protect the documents from the rain. He looked back and saw a car pulling up outside the S and D building. Security men; he was getting away just in time. He accelerated his pace.

He reached the car dripping wet and half-dizzy from the running, unlocked it, climbed inside. He clicked on the ignition, waited a moment for the turbogenerator to deliver some energy, and drove off. Flaherty lived on Riverside Drive and 89th. He hoped there wasn't much crosstown traffic.

There was no sign of the Security car behind him as he drove. At least, not for the first few minutes. But he saw the car come into view as he reached East 96th Street and turned right onto the Crosstown Skyway, and knew he was being followed.

The Skyway had a minimum speed of seventy. He jammed the accelerator down hard, pushed up above seventy-five. The needle on the speedometer approached the eight and the zero. The car back of him kept pace.

He swerved off the Skyway suddenly at the Amsterdam Avenue turn-off, doubled back to Columbus, then shot down to 88th Street through the side-streets. Rain and darkness combined to make driving rough. He drove westward along 88th, made a sharp right at West End, and cruised down 89th toward Riverside Drive, conscious that he was going the wrong way on a one-way street and hoping that nobody would decide to travel eastward on 89th at that moment.

No one did. He sprang from the car and headed for the apartment building on the corner. Apparently he had lost his pursuers, at least long enough to reach Flaherty.

A shingle on the side of the building said *Harrison M. Flaherty, Ambassador Extraordinary to the United Nations from the United States of America.* Kennedy did not bother to read the small print. As soon as he saw the neat block letters that said *Harrison M. Flaherty,* he knew he had come to the right place.

Just inside the door someone in the uniform of an attendant said, "Who is it you would like to see, please?"

Kennedy caught the man staring at him strangely and

was conscious that he hardly looked impressive, soaked as he was by rain and sweat. His heart was pounding so hard he could hardly talk. He managed to say, "Am—Ambassador Flaherty."

The doorman scowled imperiously at him. Kennedy felt like killing him. "Is the Ambassador expecting you?"

Kennedy nodded. "My wife's up there now. At least, I think she is. Why don't you phone upstairs and see?"

"I'll do that."

Kennedy stood to one side, keeping an eye on the front door, while the doorman picked up the house phone. "Your name, please?"

"Kennedy. Theodore Kennedy."

It seemed that the doorman's wide eyes went wider, but he said, "Will you tell Ambassador Flaherty that there's a Mr. Theodore Kennedy down here to see him." Pause. "What? It's all right? Very well. I'll send him up."

The doorman pointed. "Elevator over there. Sixteenth floor."

Kennedy smiled ironically. "Thanks for the help, friend." He rang for the elevator and punched 16.

On the way up he leaned against the elevator wall, gasping for breath. Moisture streamed down his face. He pushed his hair out of his eyes.

The elevator stopped and Kennedy got out. He saw he was inside the foyer of one of those ultra-large apartments with private entrances. He was staring at three men in the drab uniform of the United Nations Security Police, and they were looking at him coldly, almost menacingly.

"Are you Kennedy?"

He nodded. He tried to see behind them; it seemed that some kind of party was in progress. *Did Marge get here?* he wondered.

The Security men advanced on him. He made no attempt to resist. One efficiently frisked him and relieved him of both guns, his own and Spalding's, while a second held his arms. The third relieved him of the package he carried.

"Mr. Kennedy?" a deep, calm voice said.

Kennedy looked up. He saw a bulky, impressive, gray-maned figure of a man, standing at the entrance to the small foyer and regarding him with curiosity and a faint

130

repugnance. Next to him Kennedy saw Marge, looking white-faced and frightened.

"I'm Kennedy," he said. "My wife—"

"Your wife succeeded in forcing her way in here half an hour ago, and insisted on telling me a wild and bizarre story. I was entertaining guests at the time. I will feel most resentful if the story turns out to be false."

"It's *true*," Kennedy said, trying hard not to sound like a crackpot. He took a deep breath and stared at the frowning face of the U.N. delegate. "I don't ask you to believe me on faith, Mr. Flaherty. Lock me up. Put me in custody. Only"—he nodded at the package of documents held by one of the Security men—"read those papers. That's all I ask. Just read them."

"I'll do that," he said. He glanced at the Security men. "Meanwhile, suppose you three place him under guard. And watch him. He seems to be quite elusive."

The General Assembly of the U.N. in plenary session was an impressive sight for Kennedy, especially after his night in jail. The flags of the hundred-member organization decked the hall, and above them all rose the U.N. flag—the World Flag.

Ganymede was the topic of the day, Juan Hermanos of Chile was presiding. Yesterday, it had been agreed that the Portuguese delegate would have first word at this session but after the opening gavel fell, U.S. Delegate Flaherty rose solemnly and asked for the floor.

He said, "It has been decided that Mr. Carvalho of Portugal is to speak first today. But I wish to beg that the Chair see fit to ask Mr. Carvalho to yield place to the delegation of the United States."

The parliamentary shift was accomplished; in full possession of the floor, Flaherty nodded to the assembled delegates and contined:

"The topic most frequently discussed before this organization in recent months is that of Ganymede, the moon of Jupiter, on which a colony of Earthborn men and women has been planted. This colony has been planted by the Extraterrestrial Development and Exploration Corporation, whose Mr. Bullard I see in the group before me. The work of the Corporation is well known. Applying private capital where public financing was impossible, the Corporation

131

gave mankind the key to the stars. From among its ranks were chosen the few hundred who comprise the colony on Ganymede, the colony whose privations and dangers we all have followed with such keen interest since public announcement of its existence was made last spring.

"In short the Extraterrestrial Development and Exploration Corporation has, in the past fifty years, become virtually a supranational state, with lands of its own, police of its own, now a spacefleet of its own. This sort of private enterprise is considered commendable by current standards, since we all know the officers of the Corporation have long worked in the best interests of humanity.

"But last night a visitor came to me, a young man who has been active in the task of disseminating news of the Corporation's recent programs. He brought some rather startling papers with him to show me. I have looked through them, and I can attest they are genuine. I believe it now becomes necessary to reevaluate our entire set of beliefs, not only in the matter of Ganymede but in the matter of Corporation activity in general. I would like to yield place, if it be so resolved by this body, to Mr. Theodore Kennedy, Executive Third-Level of the public relations firm of Steward and Dinoli of this city."

The formality took a moment; Kennedy was given the floor. He rose in his place at Flaherty's left, nudging the chair back clumsily. His throat felt dry. His hands, which rested on a considerable parcel, were trembling.

He stumbled his way through the prescribed salutation. The delegates were staring at him, some with curiosity, some in boredom. In the glare of the lights he managed to pick out the thick coarse face of Bullard, the Corporation's first-level man. Bullard was leaning forward; his eyes seemed to have attained demonic intensity.

Kennedy said, "These papers I hold here give documentary proof of the most wide-scale hoax ever perpetrated in modern history. But before I distribute photostatic copies to you and let you judge for yourselves, let me briefly state my qualifications for the task I now undertake, and a summary of the charges I intend to make against the Extraterrestrial Development and Exploration Corporation.

"I have been on Ganymede from July fifth to thirtieth of this year. I have seen the planet with my own eyes. I have also helped in the fabrication of this hoax.

132

"Point One: The Corporation is willfully deceiving the people of the world, making use of the Steward & Dinoli agency as its means.

"Point Two: There is not and never has been a colony of men and women on Ganymede. There is a Corporation outpost which conisted of sixteen men in Corporation employ at the time I was there.

"Point Three: The natives of Ganymede are opposed to the exploitation of their world by the Corporation or by any other Earth people, and have declared this repeatedly to the members of the outpost there.

"Point Four: The Corporation, realizing that the natives of Ganymede do not wish their continued occupation of the planet to endure, have come to the decision that a full-scale war against the intransigent Ganymedeans will be necessary in order to subdue the planet and place it fully in their control. Not even the vast resources of the Corporation are equal to the task of waging this war, nor do they want to dissipate their capital and tie up men in what quite possibly would be a guerrilla campaign of great intensity.

"Point Five: Knowing these things, the Corporation engaged the agency for which I formerly worked, charging them with the task of so manipulating and controlling the sources of news that the true nature of events on Ganymede would be concealed and that the United Nations could ultimately be induced to carry out an armed intervention in the Corporation's behalf on Ganymede. This campaign has been highly successful. I regret to confess that it was I who originated the central concept of a fictitious colony on Ganymede which would engage the sympathies of the people of Earth—a colony which is scheduled for a fraudulent annihilation on October eleventh to serve as provocation for a Corporation request for intervention by United Nations forces."

Kennedy paused. He had spoken carefully and clearly, and as he looked around he saw a triple ring of shocked and unbelieving faces. They were starting to mutter; a moment more and there might even be jeers. But he was a master of his trade, and he had timed his speech carefully.

"Perhaps you feel that these charges of mine are the nightmares of a paranoiac, despite the fact that Ambassador Flaherty has given me his seal of approval. But I have

133

prepared photostatic copies of documents which demonstrate amply the shrewd and calculating way in which the Corporation and my agency went about the business of hoodwinking an entire world. Members of the American delegation will now pass among you distributing them."

He had waited just a moment too long. A fierce-looking delegate in bright velvet robes stood up and shouted in crisp British tones, "This is an outrage, and I protest! How can such arrant nonsense be tolerated in this hall? How can—"

Kennedy ignored him. He was staring, instead, at Bullard—Bullard, whose face had grown increasingly more contorted during his speech; Bullard, who had listened in anger to the destruction of the Corporation's plans; Bullard, who sat quivering with rage, shaking with the impact of each of Kennedy's statements—

It was too late for Kennedy to duck. He could only stand and wait as he felt the bullet crash into his shoulder and heard an instant later the strange little *pop* of Bullard's weapon; then the force of the shot knocked him backward, and as he fell he saw Security men swarming down over the struggling Bullard and heard the loud bewildered shouts of the delegates—delegates who in that moment had had all reality snatched from them, who now confronted the naked core of lies that had been cloaked so long.

20

Dizzily, Kennedy attempted to rise.

He lay sprawled behind his chair, ignored for a moment in the general confusion. His shoulder seemed to be burning.

He put one hand on the edge of the table and hoisted

himself up. He knew Marge was in the gallery somewhere and he didn't want her to worry. Delegates milled about in confusion; Hermanos was pounding the gavel and roaring for order. A flock of Security men surrounded Bullard and were dragging the Corporation man away; Bullard was white-faced with rage. Probably rage at having missed me, Kennedy thought.

A quiet voice said, "Are you all right?" The voice belonged to Ambassador Flaherty.

"I think so," Kennedy said. His shoulder throbbed painfully. He glanced at it; the jacket had a round little hole in it, singed a bit about the edges, but he did not seem to be bleeding.

But suddenly he felt weak. His wobbly legs gave way and he groped for the nearest seat and sank into it. He saw the delegation aides moving down the aisles, distributing his photostats. A hum of light conversation replaced the previous agitated buzz.

Flaherty was speaking again.

"In view of the sudden attack upon Mr. Kennedy by the Corporation executive present here, I think we cannot hesitate to take action today. The shot fired at Mr. Kennedy was a tacit admission of guilt.

"I call, therefore, for a full investigation of the relationship between the Extraterrestrial Development and Exploration Corporation and Steward and Dinoli. I ask, furthermore, that the charter of the Corporation be temporarily suspended pending full investigation, and that we consider possible ways and means of establishing direct United Nations control over space travel and interplanetary colonization, in view of the highly probable event that Mr. Kennedy's evidence will prove authentic."

Kennedy smiled despite the pain. What did a bullet in the shoulder matter, more or less, as the price for what he had done?

He turned to Flaherty and started to say something. Before he could get the first word out, though, a wave of pain rippled over him, and he struggled unsuccessfully to hold on to consciousness.

For the next few moments he heard dim voices speaking somewhere above him; then he was aware that someone was lifting him. He blanked again.

When he woke he was on a plump leatheroid couch in

135

the inner office of Ambassador Flaherty. His jacket and his bloodstained shirt lay over the back of a nearby chair. He saw three or four people bending anxiously over him as he opened his eyes.

"Ah. He is awake." A pale man in medical uniform bent over him, nodding. "I am Dr. Marquis of the United Nations Medical Staff. The bullet has been removed, Mr. Kennedy. It caused trifling damage. A few days' rest until the soreness leaves, and you'll be all right again."

"Glad to hear it."

He craned his neck until he saw Flaherty. "Well? What did I miss?"

"Plenty. Things have been popping all day. The Security men paid a visit to agency headquarters and impounded enough evidence to send your former boss and his friends to the psych-squad. Bullard's in custody here for the attempt on your life. Security forces have taken positions around all Corporation buildings now, to head off the riots."

"Riots?"

"We broke the story to the papers right after you passed out. It caused quite a stir."

Kennedy smiled. "I'll bet it did. Let me see."

They brought him an afternoon edition of a newspaper. Splashed across the front page was the biggest headline he had ever seen:

GANYMEDE COLONY TERMED HOAX BY UNITED NATIONS!

On the inside pages was the story, capped by headlines of a size normally reserved for front-page news.

He skimmed quickly through it.

A New York public relations executive today blew the lid off the biggest and best-kept hoax in modern history. Testifying before the U.N. General Assembly, Theodore Kennedy, 32, of Steward and Dinoli, revealed to an astonished gathering that the colony supposedly planted on Ganymede was nothing but a public relations hoax fabricated by his agency. Kennedy charged that the Extraterrestrial Development and Exploration Corporation had hired Steward and Dinoli last April to handle the project for them.

As a dramatic climax to the exposé, W. Richardson Bullard, 53, an Executive First-Level of the Corporation, rose from his seat in the Assembly gallery and fired point-blank at Kennedy, wounding him in the shoulder. Bullard was taken into police custody.

Also rounded up were Louis Dinoli, 66, Executive First-Level of the public-relations firm, and the four second-level men of the firm, as well as ranking Corporation officials. Further investigation—"

Kennedy scanned the rest of the paper. There was a marvelous shot of Dinoli, eyes blazing satanically, being led from the S and D offices by Security men. There was a quote from him, too: *A vile traitor has struck us a mortal blow. He has violated the sanctity of our organization. We nurtured a viper in our midst for eight years.*

There was much more: pages and pages of it. Pictures of Kennedy and an amazingly accurate biography; a transcript of the entire U.N. session that day; photographs of the Corporation leaders. A long article covered the background of the Ganymede affair from the very first public release back in May, quoting significant passages from the pseudo-accounts of the pseudo-colony. An angry editorial called for prompt punishment of the offenders and more effective monitoring of the sources of news in the future to prevent repetitions of this flagrant deception.

"Dinoli never did things in a small way," Kennedy said, looking up. "His model was the twentieth-century German dictator, Hitler. Hitler always said it's harder to fool the people on the small things than on the big ones. You could always get them to believe that the continents on the other side of the world had been swallowed up by the ocean a lot easier than you could convince them that the price of meat would drop next week. So Dinoli set out to tell the world all about Ganymede. He nearly made it, too."

He handed back the newspapers. He felt very tired, too tired to think, too tired to evaluate what he had done. All he knew was that it was over now, and he wanted to rest and plan his next move.

"Take me home," he said to Marge.

He went home. Flaherty saw to it that there were U.N. people on hand to take care of him. The house hadn't been lived in for weeks, and Marge couldn't handle everything herself.

It had been a busy couple of days, he thought. The business of Gunther's charges had been mostly cleared up, and he had been cleared of Spalding's death as well.

He sent one of the U.N. people down the road to the Camerons to fetch the cat. He asked Marge to help him across the room to the sound system; he wanted to hear some music.

He wondered briefly about the consequences of what he had done. Certainly he had finished Steward and Dinoli; a lot of men who had been drawing fancy pay would be out scrambling for jobs tomorrow, if the psych-squads didn't get them. He tried to picture old Dinoli going through Personality Adjustment, and laughed; Dinoli would be a thorn for the adjusters, a regular bramble bush!

But the others—Haugen, Cameron, Presslie. Probably they would get off easily, pleading that they were mere employees and did not set agency policy. They might draw minor sentences. After that, though, their careers in public relations were just as dead as—

As his.

What do I do now?

His name would fade from the front pages in a few days. He knew too much about communications media to believe that his current notoriety would last.

And then?

Few jobs would be open for him. Potential employers would always be aware that he had turned against Dinoli, had broken into his own office late at night to secure damning evidence. No, he would not be a safe man to employ.

One other thing troubled him. He had been through three months of torture since being assigned to the Ganymede contract. So had Marge. It showed on both of them.

He had had his eyes opened. He had learned to *think*. His brief exposure to the Ganny philosophy had given him an entirely new outlook on existence. He had developed a conscience. But a man with a conscience was useless in his line of work, and he wasn't trained for any other profession. At thirty-two it was too late to start over. He had unemployed himself.

He looked at Marge and smiled.

"You forgive me, don't you, darling?" she asked him.

"Of course I do. It wasn't exactly all your fault, what you did." Ganny words rolled through his head—words of forgiveness, words of love.

He realized that he longed to finish his conversation up there. He had just been beginning, just finding out that there *was* truth and wisdom somewhere in the universe . . . and he had been learning it from those strange, methane-breathing beings on snowswept Ganymede. That was what had changed him. That was what had impelled him to break faith with Dinoli and the Corporation—the higher call of Ganymede.

The U.N. man he had sent down the road to the Camerons returned. He shrugged apologetically and said, "I'm sorry, Mr. Kennedy. The Camerons weren't home, and the neighbors said they were away and wouldn't be back for a long time. I couldn't find the cat. The man in the next house says he thinks it ran away last week."

"That's all right," Kennedy said. "Thanks."

"Oh!" Marge said. "Poor old McGillicudy!"

Kennedy nodded, listening to the solemn *marcia funebre* coming from the audio speaker. Poor old cat, he thought; after a decade, nearly, of civilized life, he had to go back to the jungle. He probably had forgotten how to catch mice after all these years.

But it was just as well. The cat was part of the past, too, and the past was dropping away, sloughing off and vanishing down the river of time.

No cat, no job, no past. And fame was fast fleeting. Today he was "The Man Who Exposed The Corporation"; tomorrow he'd be just another jobless has-been, trying to coast through life on his old press clippings. He'd seen it happen to other heroes all too often.

His mind drifted back two months, to his short stay on Ganymede. Ganymede had served as the catalyst, as it were, for the change in his life. On Ganymede . . .

Yes. He knew what he wanted.

"Marge?"

"What is it, Ted?"

"How fond are you of living on Earth?"

Her bloodshot eyes lifted slightly. "You mean—go back to—"

He nodded. He waited a moment; she smiled.

"Will you be happy there?" she asked.

"Very."

"I can't say no, can I?"

"If you don't want to go, you don't have to. But—"

She kissed his forehead lightly. "Did I say I didn't want to go?"

It had been a fine scene, a memorable one, Kennedy thought, as he relived it in his mind once again three weeks after the blast-off. It had been Saturday, December 30, 2044—the final day of the old year, and the final day on Earth for Ted and Marge Kennedy.

Spacefield Seven in New Jersey was bright with snow—the soft, fluffy, sparkling snow of Earth, not the bleak, blue-flecked, forbidding snow of Ganymede. There had been a heavy fall on Christmas Eve, and most of it still remained on the ground in the rural areas. The Bureau of Weather Adjustment had never been too good at averting snow, and Kennedy was glad of it; few things were more beautiful, he thought, than the whiteness of falling snow against the black of a winter night.

The spaceship stood tall and proud in the center of the field. Once it had been a Corporation ship; now it belonged to the United Nations. The crew was a Corporation-trained crew, but they had a new loyalty now. The November trials had finished off the Corporation.

In his mind's eye, three weeks later, Kennedy recreated the moment. Flaherty was there, and Secretary-General Isaacs, and most of the other United Nations delegates, as well as representatives from every news medium.

Kennedy stood between Flaherty and Isaacs. The Secretary-General was saying, "Your work will be terribly important to us all, Mr. Kennedy. And the peoples of the world may believe this—every word that comes to us from you will go out to humanity exactly as it is received."

The pilots had signaled. The ship was ready. Kennedy made a neat little farewell speech and walked across the snow-bright field toward the waiting ship.

Flash bulbs went off. Cameras ground.

He and Marge ascended the catwalk.

Now he thought back over those last minutes of his on Earth. They had waved to him, and he had waved back, and he had climbed aboard the ship. The crewmen showed him to his hammock with deference.

They supplied Marge and Kennedy with gravanol pills. He grinned, remembering his last experience with one, and swallowed it.

Tomorrow on Earth was going to be a day without a name, a day without a date—the Year-End World Holiday, a day of wild and frenzied joy. As he waited for blast-off, Kennedy's mind went back six months to the Leap Year World Holiday—that day of black despair, half-forgotten now.

The day after tomorrow would see a new year on Earth. And for him, a new life.

Resident Administrator of the United Nations Commission to Ganymede. It was a big title, and an even bigger responsibility. In his hands would be the task of convincing the Ganymedeans that the people of Earth would treat them as brothers. That the Corporation was not representative of all Earth.

He would have to win the respect and the admiration of the Gannys. They remembered him as the man who had been different from the others; he hoped they would continue to trust him. He had asked for and received the job of teaching the Ganymedeans to forget their first bitter experiences with the invaders from Earth. Kennedy did not doubt he would succeed; the Gannys were wise, and would listen to him. There would be an exchange of knowledge —Ganny culture for Terran technology. Kennedy would help to bring all this about.

On Earth, now, he thought as blast-off began, they were celebrating the coming of the new year, the birth of 2045 from the dead husk of 2044. It was something of a rebirth for him too, he thought; out of the Executive Third-Level of six months before, out of the mad world of public relations, had come a different man, one who had a real and valuable job to do and who was going to do it.

There were other worlds in space; perhaps someday man would meet a second intelligent race, and a third. The Ganymede experience would guide them in their future encounters.

The trip had been a smooth one. Now it was nearly over. Earth was just a hazy memory behind him. Ahead lay Ganymede, waiting.

The ship's medic appeared. "Sir?"

"What is it, Johnson?"

"We'll be entering deceleration orbit in twelve minutes, sir. I've brought gravanol pills for you and your wife."

Marge took hers, grinned, and popped the pill into her mouth. But Kennedy brushed the medic's hand away as he offered a pill to him.

"No thanks, Johnson. I want to see the whole thing."

"Ted!"

"I've been through it before, Marge. This time I want to watch."

He strapped himself in, leaned back, and peered out the port at the whiteness of Ganymede growing nearer outside. The ship began to plunge down toward its destination; Kennedy smiled calmly to himself and waited for the landing.